DUNCAN

The Prophet's Return

J W Throgmorton

ISBN-13: 978-0692526941
ISBN-10: 0692526943

DISCLAIMER

This novel is a work of fiction. Names, characters, places, and incidents either are the product of the author's imagination, or are used fictitiously. Any resemblance to actual persons, living or dead, events, or locales is entirely coincidental.

DEDICATION

Without the blessing, and patience of my bride, DJ, this book would never have happened.

Other Books by this author:

Duncan Green River (Book I)
Duncan Pirates of California (Book II)
Kilchii
Talon's Debt
Toots McGee
(Hale Publishing • London)
McGraw Returns
(Hale Publishing • London)

Visit the author's webpage:

www.jwthrogmorton.com

Prologue

Gone are the yellow glow of street lamps and the harsh flickering white light of fluorescent fixtures streaming through office windows. The twilit sky rendered only faint visibility for those who dared travel. Dark deserted high-rise structures formed walls of deep interlinking canyons, which cast eerie shadows that concealed long portions of the city's abandoned streets.

It was year one, more or less, of the 'Decline'. Those who dared to travel the streets of LoDo, Lower Downtown Denver, stayed ever vigilant in fear of those depraved inhabitants who'd remained after the deterioration of the city's civil infrastructure. It became a no man's land where life had little value, and it was survival of the strongest and unmerciful.

Loaded with sand for icy road conditions, a green one-ton Dodge Ram with bubbled paint, rusted cavities that resembled pockmarks, and missing its chrome, slowed at an intersection. Its oversized knobby tires crunched the packed snow as it rolled to a stop. The hot air blowing up from the defrosters cleared double arches of frost from the windshield. Paul had to crane his neck to see out.

Its occupants, newlyweds Paul and Vanessa Duncan, married only a few days, were trying to get back to Paul's apartment on campus, where he was an Associate Professor of Physics in the Science Department at the University of Denver. They'd met when she audited one of his lectures on classical mechanics. It was her freshman year, and she wondered if she had an interest in physics. She didn't, but she did like the freckle faced red-headed professor, and continued to attend his lectures. Eventually, Paul realized the attractive young woman wasn't formally part of his class ….

At full alert, the couple watched for other vehicles. The truck's heater blew hot air from beneath the dash, but its warmth never rose above the bench seat. Red circles formed on Vanessa's white cheeks, and her breath fogged the cab as she spoke, "There's a car coming." The apprehensiveness in her voice was nearly palpable.

Her pale-blue eyes were fixed on the movement coming from the shadows at the rights side of the intersection.

"I see it, Sweetie." He downshifted and shook his long hair away from his green eyes to clear his vision. For the thousandth time on this trip, he glanced at the dashboard to confirm what he already knew; the truck's gear selector remained in four-wheel-drive.

A black Cadillac limo crept from the darkness like a panther prowling its territory on the hunt. As it neared, the driver's window slowly lowered. Paul saw its occupants were rough looking men. The couple could clearly read the malevolence in his dark sinister eyes. He looked first at Paul and then Vanessa.

When Paul saw the car's brake indicator lights brighten, he instantly knew they were in danger. "Hang on," he yelled and stomped the gas. Before the limousine could fully stop, Paul's truck leapt through the intersection gaining speed as they pulled away.

Vanessa glanced at him for reassurance, and then she turned and stared through the rear window. Her woolen scarf slipped away and fell to her shoulders exposing her long blonde hair.

Unconsciously, she reached out and clutched at the sleeve of Paul's jacket. "Oh, Paul," she cried. "What're we going to do?"

Paul watched in his side mirror; the limo raced after them. He glanced at Vanessa and saw her eyes wide with fear. "Just hang on, Sweetie. It'll be OK—I promise." Vanessa turned back in her seat and belted in; she clutched the leather pull mounted above the door, and squeezed her eyes shut. Paul heard her muttering a prayer.

Deserted vehicles and snow banks restricted the road's passage to a single lane. Paul knew he had the advantage, which increased his confidence of their escape. Quickly, he hazarded another glance at Vanessa. Even in the fading light, he could see her terrified expression. "When we get to the freeway, we're home free," he said, with the intent to quell her panic.

He checked his mirror and saw one of the men animatedly speaking into a handheld two-way radio. Vanessa, who now also watched the road, noticed Paul's focus on the rearview mirror. She turned her head to check the limo's progress. When she too saw the man with the radio, she asked, "What's he doing?"

"It can't be good," said Paul, as he turned onto Twenty-Second Street headed for the freeway's on-ramp. "Shit," cursed Paul. His voice filled with alarm and pounded his fist on the steering wheel. The road ahead was blocked by two yellow school buses parked back-to-back.

Close behind them the limousine blocked any chance of retreat leaving them nowhere to go. "Paul, do something," screamed Vanessa, terror twisted her expression as she clutched his arm. Finally, looking away, she covered her eyes.

Paul ignored her screams and focused on the buses. He plotted the situation, and made hasty calculations. His decision made, he gave his only warning to Vanessa, "Hang on," he said and sped up the truck. He gripped the steering wheel as his eyes flickered between the yellow buses and the speedometer; fifty—sixty—seventy miles per hour.

As his speed began to increase, two men, dressed in parkas and armed with rifles, casually emerged from the five-foot space between the rears of the buses. The taller man on Paul's left boldly raised his hand, the universal sign to halt. Paul raised the middle finger of his right hand, defiantly signaling his reply.

Everything moved in slow motion. Vanessa screamed and gripped the pull strap, her knuckles bulging against her leather gloves. The expression on the faces of the two men began to change from arrogance to terror, as they realized the truck did not plan to stop. A smile creased Paul's face at the spectacle of the two guards diving into snow banks to get out of the way.

It was basic physics, or so he hoped. His truck's weight plus the sand he carried traveling at over seventy miles per hour should produce enough force to punch through between the buses.

On impact, momentum launched them frontward inside the vehicle. Their safety belts strained against their bodies for a split second as the truck hesitated. Then the inert mound of sand in the bed of the truck, still traveling at seventy miles per hour, shifted. Its force propelled the truck forward slamming them back into their seats. The impact bent the Ram's reinforced steel bumper as the buses swung apart like giant yellow gates.

Paul would never forget the deafening sound of crunching metal and breaking glass, or the carbon taste and odor of steel grinding against steel. He stole a quick glance in his mirror and smiled when he saw the limousine's driver half out of his vehicle staring after them. The driver shook his head and didn't give pursuit. He must have thought them crazy and too dangerous to chase.

Rattling and banging a great deal more than before, Paul's truck delivered them safely to a friend's house. There they intended to stay for the next several days and make plans for their future.

***

One year earlier ….

It was late August; the summer sun blazed hot during the day. Driving on an old black topped road, appearing through the shimmer of heat waves traveled a convoy of battered trucks. Crumpled fenders, broken windows, and bullet holes punched neatly through its sheet metal tell of battles already fought. Seething men and women seeking retribution filled the vehicles. The lead truck halted in front of a chalky white road-sign that stood sentinel at the edge of town. Its faded black letters announced to all:

> Farmington, Illinois
> Founded: 1834
> Population: 1,624.

In the bed of the truck stood a disheveled drunkard, his long brown hair and unshaven face were grimy with road grit. White rings enclosed dark circles of perspiration that spread from his armpits. Like tree rings, their number counted the days since his last bath. He squinted to focus his eyes on the sign's words and sneered at what the sign represented: 'hope and prosperity'. His shotgun swayed in the air as he aimed and fired. Its blast reverberated across the serene farmland. As the truck moved passed the sign, he saw where the pellets tore through the metal destroying the words. He smiled without humor.

Farmington's courthouse square lay at the center of town framed by colonnades of tall oak trees. The community visited the square every Saturday to socialize and conduct business. The people who meandered about the square stopped when they heard a terrified woman's scream. Their eyes followed the direction of her pointing, and watched as a caravan of trucks roared into town and surrounded the square. Forty looters armed with semiautomatic rifles, shotguns, and pistol looked back with menacing stares.

The gang descended on Farmington like a plague. They came from Hanna City where they spent three-days looting and killing. The marauders no longer feared that the civil authorities would, or even could, intervene. Just weeks earlier, these despoilers were members of a friendly hardworking neighborhood of law-abiding citizens in Peoria. Despite their ever-growing plight, they desperately tried to maintain normal lives. "Things would be better soon," people said. "It has to be—that's what the Government promised."

Day by day, their frustrations grew; lost jobs, empty store shelves, water and power turned off. Even so, they continued to believe in and followed the rule of law. Their allegiance broke when Evelyn and Michael Larson brought Mary, their four-year-old daughter, home from the doctor. Delirious, soaking wet with sweat, and her temperature critical; had it been available, antibiotics would have cured her minor infection.

Six-hours later, Mary, the neighborhood's little blonde angel, whom all adored, died leaving Michael Larson to question, "How can this happen?" Numbed by heartache and confused, he knelt beside her body filled with anguish. Tears fell from his normally clear brown eyes; now rubbed red, he moaned, "It was only an infection." He beseeched his wife for an answer, "People don't die from that, especially, one so young and healthy like her." Herself stricken with grief; his wife offered no answer.

Michael stormed out of his house. Like his neighbors, he lived in a clapboard sided bungalow built in the forties. He stopped when he saw Mary's pink bicycles fixed with training wheels standing idle in the front yard. He knelt beside it and stroked the streamers hanging from the handlebar grips. Mary's favorite doll rested in the white wicker basket. Its eyes open; staring at nothing.

Crazed from heartbreak, he ran his bony fingers through his dark tousled hair and then swiped at his unshaven face. He looked up and found gathered on the street, his neighbors. They waited to hear news of Mary's condition. In a grief-stricken rage, he began to rail, "Mary's dead." The crowd went silent, "The doctor didn't have any medicine, nor knew where to find any." Tears streamed down his tortured face as he continued.

"I've had enough. The government can't, or won't help us. They make sure the fat-cats, and their cronies are taken care of, but we are left to fend for ourselves." Looking about the crowd, he saw heads nodding, "I say we band together and take what we need." Michael's anger and his words of contempt for his city, the government, even his country, and its leadership were contagious. In those few moments, Michael Larson spawned rebellion and the beginning of the end.

It was a hot July day. They were hungry; they didn't understand why things weren't being taken care of; they were afraid. Larson's words soothed their fear. He proposed action; a way to return the things they'd lost. They gathered their weapons and drove to the heart of the city.

They'd been deprived too long, but no more. Once constituting a bastion of suburban bliss, they were now intent on taking by any means necessary what they believed rightfully theirs. Looting from store-to-store, they found the proprietors undefended and surprised. Soon, others followed their example and started pillaging, too.

Ultimately, they encountered armed resistance from business owners defending their stores, and rival gangs protecting their turf. In a fight with another group, they lost two of their number. Over the next few days the city's population separated into two types; gangs bent on looting and senseless destruction, or proprietors protecting their property. Skirmishes soon became a daily occurrence and factions grafted together increasing their security. Makeshift compounds began to appear.

During a respite from their rampage Albert Evans, a tall middle-aged man with grey hair and a beer belly, and a twenty-year veteran of a local factory, voiced his opinion on what they should do next. From the rooftop of his truck, he shouted, "We should move on to the farmlands where people are more self-reliant. They're sure to have plenty of food." Albert having an opinion, by default, made him their leader.

Few tried to stop them … the Decline of the United States as a nation began with anarchy spawned in Peoria, Illinois.

***

Global warming, an earth killer asteroid, World War III, or even a great plague—any of these seemed more plausible as a beginning of the End. No one expected the total collapse of the world's economy, or that it would be the mechanism for the decline of the world's civilizations.

Bank closings became epidemic. The ones that did not initially close would not lend. Without capital, businesses failed and unemployment soared. The world's governments continued to print money to keep their economies afloat, but in the end, their currencies lost all value.

Finally, even precious metals and gems became worthless. Only the things that people could eat, drink, or wear had value. Hoarding food had become essential and salt became the sole currency accepted for trade.

The Decline, at its beginning spread slowly, until one city service after another disappeared. Eventually, water and electricity ceased and then firefighters, police, and ambulances stopped responding. Violence once it began became impossible to end.

Governors requested the Federal Military when anarchy broke out, but the troops never came. They stayed home to protect their own families. World conflicts wound down to local skirmishes since the countries involved did not have the wherewithal to continue fighting. The demise of global transportation and communications stranded countless travelers never to return home.

Small rural towns became the last bastions of civilization. At first, their citizens persevered to keep towns operating; to maintain a sense of community. However, after waves of looters attacked, they banded together and built forts for their protection and turned away strangers.

The first years were horrifying; millions died from starvation and neglect followed by pestilence. Western civilizations suffered the greatest losses. Earth's population dropped to less than sixty percent within the first ten years.

Pockets of technology would endure for a few decades. People used natural fuels to produce electricity until they had depleted the supplies. Nuclear power plants provided electricity until the distribution grids failed. Eventually, there was no one left, who knew how to maintain the equipment, and the radiation from the meltdowns destroyed massive areas of the earth's surface. Hydroelectric power held on the longest, but without maintenance even that failed.

Gangs controlled the outskirts of cities, raiding the commercial centers for food. In due course, they consumed the available food stores and then rumors surfaced of cannibalism.

Civilizations of the world became reminiscent of Europe's dark ages. Basic education survived, higher learning, especially the sciences, did not. Yet, for some there remained a hope that a new renaissance would emerge from the world's lost knowledge. That 'It' lies just under the surface like a dormant seed; waiting….

DUNCAN The prophet's return

Chapter 1

More than a year ago, Josh Duncan left Denver to explore the Pacific seacoast. Leaner now, Duncan still remained thick with muscle; muscle born from long-hours of strenuous work. The kind of work that forges endurance far beyond that tolerated by his animals; save Lucky, his wolf companion.

He'd promised his family to be home within eighteen-months. It should have been enough time to have made the trip twice; however, the troubles he encountered at Green River, Wyoming, and the months he spent as a pirate captive put his travel plans behind schedule. The recent message of Mary's kidnapping canceled his plans entirely. His fiancée's safe return consumed his thoughts. With no idea of when he'll return home, he knew his family would soon become concerned; no time to worry about them now. He rode on.

The sunlight that caused Duncan's green eyes to squint in the morning and warmed his broad back in the afternoon faded behind clouds of smoky grey with swirls of purple and orange. In the saddle since first light, he'd pushed his animals at a pace far harder than he liked, but he needed to get back to New Lovelock. He had to find out what's happened to Mary. He glanced down at his horse's head. It pumped up and down, and the horse lunged forward with each step. Lathered from exertion, Buck needed rest and water; it was time to halt for the day.

Ten-miles east of Truckee, California, Duncan followed the remnants of Highway 80. Its asphalt pavement disintegrated in most places; weakened by the sun's ultraviolet rays and the freeze-thaw cycles. The remains cracked resembling the skin of an ancient alligator. Pine trees encroach onto the road; soon the road would be gone completely, and future travelers would have to forge a new path across the mountains.

Ahead, Duncan saw a concrete overpass. It too began to decay; exposed steel reinforcement protruded where great chunks broke free from the structure. He'd camp there tonight. At over 5,000-foot elevation, it would be cold at night. A campfire next to one of the concrete abutments would create a heat-sink that would radiate warmth throughout the night.

As he rode down the off-ramp, he could see what lay under the bridge. On the east side of the road, a small stream of clean water flowed; further on laid the steel rails of an abandoned railroad. Under the bridge, Duncan set to work taking care of his animals. Buck, his dappled-grey gelding, and Alice and Sophie his two mollies; matched mules.

Duncan scooped up a palm full of water. It tasted clean and sweet; he looked forward to a hot cup of coffee. After seeing to Buck and the girls, he climbed the sloped concrete abutment. Atop, he found soft dry soil. He saw the remains of old campfires and salvaged rocks for his fire ring. Past travelers left railroad ties pulled from the tracks on the far side of the stream. After a short search for kindling, he soon had a fire and coffee brewing; a hot meal of rice and beans followed.

Finished with cleaning his cookware, he boiled water to have a sponge bathed. Feeling refreshed and very relaxed, Duncan sipped the last of the coffee. He resisted the temptation of adding a dram of whiskey. He was already yawning; he'd sleep well without it.

A half-circle of heavy black-soot six-foot wide on the concrete footing absorbed much of the light radiating from the fire, but there remained enough for Duncan to see. Matt Wade, his friend and militiaman from New Lovelock, left a message for him with Molly. She owned the boarding house where he stayed in San Francisco. As he remembered his friend; a brief smile softened his face as he recalled Matt's desire to court Jane, Mary's younger sister.

Duncan lost count of how many times he'd read the message in the last three days. With his calloused hands, he carefully unfolded the message. It read: 'Duncan, Mary's been taken. Her sisters are safe, but they need you. Sorry to be the barer of such bad news, your friend Matt.' His friend's tersely worded note left Duncan with many questions. Questions his imagination attempted to answer and created the worse of scenarios for what could have happened.

Self-reproach lingered in his mind and tugged at his heart. If he lost Mary because he wanted to leave on his adventure, he'd never forgive himself. Mary wanted to come with him, but he refused to allow it; maybe, he should have stayed and married her and forgotten about his plans. At least then, he could have protected her, and her sisters. Images of Jane and the twins, Helen and Sarah, cycled through his mind.

Lucky, his wolf companion crawled into light of the fire. He seemed to understand Duncan's need for solace. He whined and inched closer placing his huge furry head on Duncan's leg. The wolf lay there for several minutes. As if being called, he lifted his nose to the wind, and then jumped to all fours. He issued a low, "Gruff," and loped out of camp.

Duncan called, "Good hunting, Boy." He glanced towards Buck and the girls and added, "We won't see him 'til morning."

Duncan sighed, finished his coffee, and crawled into his sleeping bag for much-needed sleep. Old, the bag was made of synthetic materials and weathered the time well. With his boots within reach and his jacket used as a pillow, Duncan kept warm and dry.

Like the three nights before, Duncan slept fitfully; it was a reoccurring nightmare. In the dream, John Kimball, the religious zealot known as The Leader to his followers, is chasing Mary across the great salt flats. He sees Kimball as a lean shadowy figure dressed in black with long tangled hair and beard. His crazed dark eyes are sunken into his skull surrounded with charcoal colored circles. He reaches out for Mary nearly snatching her away. Duncan can see what is about to happen, but is powerless to stop it. He awakens with Svengali or Rasputin like images swirling across his mind. It was one of the few times he resented his life of books and reading; where else could those images have come from?

With his heart still pounding, he sat up, and ran his sun-burnt freckled hands through his sandy-colored hair. He paused to examine its thickness and thought; I could use a haircut. Reaching, he picked up and knocked the dirt off his brimmed leather hat and crammed it on his head. Scratching the stubble on his face, he said aloud, "I guess a shave wouldn't hurt anything either." Buck's head came up; he neighed at the sound of his rider's voice.

Duncan crawled from his sleeping bag, stoked the fire's embers and added fuel. Soon, he had coffee brewing and went to check on his animals. The saddling and packing process started every day on the trail. He paused, and looked about—where was Lucky? This was a first. It was rare that he woke without the wolf curled at his feet, but he certainly showed up by the time his coffee brewed. He called, "Lucky—Lucky, you out there, Boy?"

Though he wasn't worried, he was curious; what would keep Lucky away from camp? Had he been unable to catch his meal? Duncan continued with his morning routine. By the time he was ready to ride, Lucky still hadn't appeared; now Duncan worried.

With an eye on the tree line, Duncan eased onto the highway. He'd start out at a walk to get his animals warmed up and then increase to a canter. A few miles down the road, he saw Lucky. At least, he thought it was Lucky, but if it was he, he wasn't alone. There was a smaller wolf loping alongside Lucky. Duncan smiled; it was a she-wolf.

Duncan watched them as they loped along. Every time Lucky drifted toward the road, the female drew back. Lucky followed to coax her forward keeping pace with Duncan, Buck, and the girls. Hour after hour Lucky slowly moved him and his mate closer until they ran alongside Duncan and his animals. It was Duncan's first close look at the she-wolf. She had a white face with dark fur below her eyes like shadows. "Shadow will be your name," he mumbled under his breath.

More out of curiosity than fatigue, he decided to make camp earlier than usual. Duncan wanted a chance to entice Lucky's new friend, his mate, into their camp for a formal meeting. For that, he needed fresh meat.

As if on cue, a young black-tailed doe stood staring at them transfixed in the center of the road. Duncan judged the deer was seventy-five yards away. Slowly, he eased his carbine to his shoulder, released his breath, and fired. Several things happened simultaneously: Buck startled, and side stepped; the deer jumped straight up and then fell; the girls tugged on their reins trying to pull away, and Shadow bolted for cover.

"Whoa there," called Duncan as he gained control of his animals. A glance at Lucky revealed the wolf's displeasure. He turned and trotted off after his new mate. After a good chuckle, Duncan said aloud, "I guess, I should've thought that through more—"

He rode to the kill; the deer was down, but not dead. Years of hunting had not lessened the sadness he felt at having to dispatch game at close range. Duncan un-holstered the Colt .45 revolver; he carried as a saddle gun when traveling. Dismounting, he stepped to the doe. Duncan stared; the confused innocence he saw in her eyes reminded him of the night Mary, and her sisters entered his campfire light. They sought food and shelter; and hoped he would save them, which he did. Even when Kimball followed them to New Lovelock, he kept them safe.

Only after he abandoned them was Kimball able to take her. The last showdown, when he'd wounded Kimball and the fanatic escaped, he should have made sure Kimball was dead—Buck neighed, interrupting his thoughts. He looked around as if unsure how he'd gotten there. The deer tried to rise; the muscles along his jaw flexed with determination as he aimed. He fired a single shot. She flinched once and then lay still. Her eyes dulled as her life ended.

Duncan selected an area near the tree-line for his campsite, and dragged the deer's carcass to one of the trees. Suspended from a tree limb, he cleaned and carved the meat. On a spit suspended over the campfire, he roasted a hindquarter. The rest of the carcass, he lowered to the ground and left for Lucky and his mate; hoping their hunger would win out.

Lucky approached straight away and tore into the deer's flesh, but Shadow held back. Finally, as he hoped, she timidly came forward and ripped free a chuck of meat, and then scurried a safe distance away to eat it. Soon, however, she stood next to Lucky and ate her fill.

Duncan studied the wolf; she was younger and maybe twenty pounds lighter than Lucky. Her eyes were green in contrast to Lucky's golden amber color. Overall, he decided she was attractive and, in human terms, understood why Lucky chose her.

After Lucky ate, he came and lay next to Duncan, who petted his companion and scratched behind his ears. Shadow looked on, but declined to move closer. Duncan spoke, his voice soft and low, "She's a looker, Boy. Is she just a passing fancy, or is this something long-term?" Lucky looked at him, his expression serious, at least that's what Duncan saw. "Oh, right—wolves' mate for life, so I guess it's long-term then." He chuckled at his humor.

Shadow rose and began to pace expectantly. Lucky stood, gave Duncan a quick glance and trotted over to his mate, and together they loped off into the woods. They left Duncan alone with his thoughts, which soon drifted back to his last encounter with Kimball and his guards.

With Kimball's guards down, or captured, Duncan moved to execute Kimball. As he closed, the Leader read the intent in Duncan's eyes and put his hands up. Sanity flashed across his face as he realized he was to die. "—but I surrender," he cried.

As Duncan raised his weapon to fire, Robert, Kimball's chief guard, though wounded, grabbed Duncan's leg and caused his shot to go wide. The shot struck the crazed zealot in the arm. Wounded, Kimball stumbled into the tall grass while Duncan dealt with Robert. Lucky pursued Kimball; Duncan heard Kimball's screams, and assumed Lucky had killed him. When Duncan caught up with Lucky, his muzzle was blood soaked. They stood by a fast-moving stream, with no Kimball in sight. He and the wolf searched but didn't find Kimball's body, or if he survived where he left the water. Duncan mistakenly assumed Kimball drowned, or worse.

Matt and the militia delivered Kimball's guards to New Lovelock. There, under martial-law presided over by Col. Marcus Atkin, the militia commander, they were tried and convicted of kidnapping and attempted murder; and then hanged. To their credit, none of them begged for mercy.

One of the mollies brayed bringing Duncan back to the present. He stood and walked to where they and Buck were hobbled. There was grass, but no water. Using his hat, he poured water into it for each in turn giving them a drink before turning in. As he crawled into his bag, he briefly wondered if he'd see

Lucky the next morning.

After another night of fitful sleep, Duncan still rose at first light. For the second morning, Lucky was nowhere to be seen. He frowned, but wasn't surprised; he began to wonder if he would ever see his friend again. He always felt that one-day the wolf would leave to have a life in the wild, but now? If he was to find Mary, he would need Lucky's help.

Travel for the next three-days was much the same as the day before. Duncan no longer searched for Lucky as he rode. He felt abandoned when Lucky didn't return; the emotion surprised him. The time he and Lucky remained apart in San Francisco, while held captive by Taras didn't seem like a loss only a temporary separation. Though he understood the wolf might give up waiting for his return, Duncan never felt the heartbreak of being deserted by his friend.

If he was to find Mary, it would be without Lucky.

Chapter 2

Dressed wholly in black, John Kimball stood on the chapel's rostrum; sunlight streamed through a skylight above causing him to resemble a featureless specter. He was a sharp contrast to the monochromous white background often used in the decoration of Mormon Temples. Only the natural color of the hardwood used to construct the pews, and the sky blue carpet deviated. Even its members dressed in white or subdued colors when they attended a sermon inside the temple. Kimball felt his unique state with God gave him the privilege to ignore the church's tenets.

John's grandfather, and his namesake, declared him a Virginal Birth of his daughter, sired by an angel sent by God. Furthermore, he claimed him as God's Prophet on earth? The genuinely devoted of their compound accepted the dogma as gospel. However,

there are many who suspected John the elder
incestuously fathered him.

Kimball's grandfather was a young man when
the Decline began. He saw it as God's retribution
against the non-believers and founded his compound
based on the strictest doctrines' of the church; adding
his unique interpretations when needed to further his
desires. He found it relatively easy to recruit follows.
People were confused and afraid; Kimball offered a
reason why the Decline happened. To gain their
salvation and protection, his followers had to accept
his doctrines.

Kimball, senior took eight-wives; his appetite for
lust never truly satisfied. Through his numerous
matings, he only produced one child, with wife
number eight, a daughter, who he named Josephine.
He doted on her and when she was sixteen, she too
became pregnant.

Though many suspected John's grandfather was
the father, especially his wives, none made any
accusations. Senior didn't interact with his incestuous
offspring until after the boy reached the age of five.

His grandfather denied John playmates, and
personally saw to the boy's education. He taught the
boy from the Book of Mormons modified with Senior's

unique interpretations. Senior's wives and young John's mother did not interfere. They were so grateful he no longer plagued them; they were willing to forfeit the child.

The boy spent each day with his namesake. His existence soon became commonplace; to the point that he went unnoticed by the compound's occupants. Even so, the young boy took notice of them. He witnessed how people treated his grandfather. People of the compound bowed their heads, or averted their eyes. Some knelt to receive his blessing.

By age ten, young John began preaching to the stable animals. His belief that he was truly a prophet of God had become irretrievably cast. Those still a child, John's stare held sway over those who opposed his or his grandfather's will. The signs that his sanity was in jeopardy were ignored. Even when his grandfather found him standing in front of their rabbit hutch where he'd strangled a doe and was trying to bring it back to life. Senior excused the matter as childish exuberance, and killed two more rabbits for dinner.

Unchecked, his cruelty, continued towards animals and eventually people. A young girl went missing from the compound. Senior discovered John in the barn with her raped and mutilated body. Senior disposed of the body, and then he beat the boy mercilessly with a leather strap. "If you are to one-day rule this compound, you must not compromise me, or yourself," he said. "If the people found out what you've done it would cause a revolt—do you understand?"

Though severely beaten, the sixteen-year-old boy shed not a single tear. The lesson he learned was never again be discovered.

***

Kimball gestured toward the blonde young woman dressed in a cream-colored linen gown. She sat erect on a white velvet covered chair on the rostrum beside him. His long sinewy fingers seemed to grow from the sleeve of his left arm. It was an animated contrast to his right arm; amputated at the elbow. A self-performed task to insure his survival after he'd escaped from the militia led by Joshua Duncan, who also stole his bride.

It was Duncan who defied Kimball's prophecy. God spoke to Kimball and told him that he would wed each of the Evans sisters in turn as they flowered. When he thought of the prophecy, it nearly always transformed into a lust filled fancy. His loins quickened the strongest whenever he thought of the twins; Helen and Sarah.

As he preached, he raised his arms. His right arm stopped at the elbow. Sight of the stump caused his mind to burn with the desire for vengeance. He had surrendered, but Duncan shot him anyway. The bullet from Duncan's gun shattered the bone and caused the loss of Kimball's arm; and Duncan's tamed wolf from hell scarred his face. One day, one day soon, he would have his revenge.

Kimball's stringy black hair covered the right side of his mauled partially bearded face; though healed, his scars remain pink and tender to the touch. The disfigured tissue no longer stretched and made his speech awkward and sometimes difficult to understand, but he refused to let his condition hinder him. When he spoke his voice reverberated off the hard surfaces of the chapel. "Children, my promised bride has returned, and the prophecy shall be fulfilled."

"Amen," responded his faithful; they spoke as one. Kimball watched as his followers swayed in mass. He understood that his words gave them solace. His eyes closed, and a crooked smile creased half his face. The source of his bliss came from his followers as they voiced their cerebration of his words. The visual effect his smile created, however, was an evil sneer.

John Kimball, the 'Leader' to his followers, months earlier left his compound with five of his guard in search of Mary Evans and her sisters. He returned alone; wounded and near death, his face mutilated. Most of his acolytes considered it God's intervention that that he still lived.

The girls fled their compound when they learned of John Kimball's plan to force them to be his brides. Starving and alone, they found Joshua Duncan. He sheltered them, and killed to protect them from the guards Kimball sent to search for them. Eventually, they arrived in New Lovelock and began fresh lives.

***

Mary Evans, the girl seated on the platform next to the Leader, wore her blonde hair pulled back into a ponytail. Her blue eyes cast downward void of interest with her surroundings, or the activity that transpired next to her. Mary did not hear Kimball's rant to the inane souls who stared at them. Her mind, instead, focused on recalling the arduous details of her capture and the long journey back to her place of birth; Henefer.

The Henefer compound was once a small remote town named for the two brothers who founded it in 1858. Located northeast of Salt Lake City, her birthplace held no fond memories; even before her parents disappeared, she couldn't recall many pleasant times spent there. How long has it been since they kidnapped me, she asked herself? As she looked down at her hand, she ticked off the weeks with her fingers. Nearly nine-weeks she thought. It seemed longer, but then it also seemed like only yesterday that she was home with Jane and the twins in New Lovelock. Her mind drifted ….

Listless, Mary glanced up from the table when her second sibling, Jane, peeked into the kitchen from the hall. Jane, a younger version of Mary with the same blonde hair and blue eyes set in a pale longish, but attractive, face. Her fitted shirt-waist dress defined her youthful figure; something she'd become more aware of in recent months.

They lived in a two-bedroom mid-twentieth century white clapboard bungalow. It was built in a time when the front porch was a major part of community living; a place where they now often set drinking coffee or tea. It'd been their home since their arrival to New Lovelock. It's where she agreed to wait for Duncan while he ventured out to explore the West Coast.

In 1868, George Lovelock provided the land for the railroad to build its station, so they named the depot after him and the town that soon followed. Before the Decline, Lovelock was a sleepy farming community. Their geographic isolation allowed them to maintain a pre-Decline existence … of sorts. Attitudes about the world and strangers passing through were different there; generally, they're welcomed.

"Mary," called Jane from her room, "Martha's invited us to dinner. We haven't seen the twins for more than a minute at a time this last week—I miss them."

Mary's elbows rested on their breakfast table. She and Jane salvaged it from one of the abandoned houses on the outskirts of town, which was how they procured most of their furniture. The neglected table and chairs were pretty shabby, but their enthusiasm and hard work, along with some white paint, soon had them gleaming like new. She lowered her head and rubbed her temples. Finally, she sighed, and said, "You go on without me, Jane. I'm really tired and want to go to bed early. Tomorrow's Saturday, tell the twins to come over here, and we'll all spend the day together."

Jane entered the kitchen. Her posture reminded Mary of their mother; her arms crossed, and her jaw clinched ready for an argument. "That'll pacify them, but what about Martha and Marcus?" asked Jane. "We haven't even seen them in passing lately. You know Martha will pick at me wanting to know what's wrong with you. I'll have to tell her something."

With a weak smile, Mary said, "Don't say anything in front of Helen and Sarah—it'll upset them for no reason."

Jane Evans, the ever-blunt speaking sibling, who always states exactly what's on her mind said, "Mary, it's only a dream. The Leader is dead; you heard what Josh said. There is no way he could have survived after losing all that blood. He drowned in the river."

"—but it's so real," argued Mary. As she stared off into space, she wrapped her arms her around her body and continued. "I'm asleep and then an awareness that someone else is in my room wakes me. It's still night, but the moon is full and from the shadows steps a figure. I sit up to see who it is—"

Mary paused and involuntarily tightened her arms. Her voice is choked with fear as a hoarse cry passes her lips. "—it's The Leader!"

Jane heard Mary recite the vivid aspects of this dream several times before. For her, it was like hearing a ghost story. As Mary shared the macabre details, Jane found herself drawn into the tale. She startled when Mary cried, '—it's The Leader!' "Well you certainly make it sound real enough. No wonder you're not sleeping." Jane turned to exit, hesitated, and then looked back. "You know—having dinner at with Atkins' might help take your mind off the dream. You could excuse yourself early."

Mary glanced at Jane and saw the pleading in her eyes. She shook her head and let out a sigh. "Maybe you're right—give me a minute to freshen up."

At the Atkins' home, Helen and Sarah greeted them at the door. Identical twins, the younger sisters were matching bookends of Mary and Jane. Until recently, they always dressed alike and enjoyed the fun of trying to confuse people as to which one was which. However, since achieving teenage status and signs of womanhood began to show, boys are their main topic of their conversations; and neither wished to be mistaken as the other.

Martha and Marcus Atkins took the twins in when the girls first arrived in New Lovelock. Childless themselves, the girls became belated treasures to the couple. Martha's thin rawboned body contrasted Marcus's rotund figure. Though, he attended temple with Martha, he was not as devout as she wished, but they are a happy loving couple who have found great joy living with the twins. With gentle guidance from the Atkins', Helen and Sarah quickly adjusted to their new home. It's been nearly a year now, and like most teenagers, they take their good luck for granted.

Sarah took Mary's hand, and Helen grabbed Jane's. Together the twins whisked their elder sisters into the kitchen where Martha prepared dinner. The room is a small space just large enough for a breakfast table covered with a patterned table cloth once belonging to Martha's mother. Marcus sat at the far end near the back door and sipped coffee. He sifted through the documents spread across the table; they related to the militia of which he commanded.

Martha turned to the noise of giggling girls. Her grey hair tussled, and her face red from standing over the stove, Martha beamed when Mary and Jane entered the room. "My, it seems like ages since you've come for dinner." She paused to look at them closer inspecting them from head to toe. "Both of you are too skinny—it's not healthy."

Marcus sat down his cup, gathered up the documents, and set them aside to make room for the girls at the table. "Martha, stop fussing at them, they look just fine. Why, every young man in the community has their eye on Jane."

"That's all well and good, but young women need to have some meat on their bones—it's healthier."

"So you've said, dear. They can fatten up once they're married. Speaking of marriage, Jane, I've been seein' you and Matt together a lot—"

Color flared to Jane's cheeks, and the twins closed in like wolves circling a wounded prey. "Oh, Jane," said Sarah, the first to pounce. "Matt Wade is the most handsome man in New Lovelock. Are you going to marry him?"

Helen chimed in, "Well, are you?"

The blush in her cheeks now burned with indignation, and she barked. "Stop pestering me, you two—he hasn't asked me yet."

Undeterred, Helen persisted. "Is he seeing another girl? I'm sure we would've heard if he is."

Martha stepped in. "Girls, please set the table."

"Oh, Aunt Martha," said Sarah, "we just want to know if—"

Interrupting, Martha said, "Of course, she's going to marry some fine young man, and it'll happen in its own good time. Meanwhile, leave your sister alone on the subject."

Marcus' brow furrowed and his head tilted to the left. A concerned tone entered his voice. "Jane, I could speak to Wade. I mean, if he's not contemplating marriage, he should step aside and give the other young men a chance."

Jane's eyes went wide, and her mouth gaped. She recovered fast, but her protest was quick and fervid. "Oh no, Uncle Marcus, please don't say anything to Matthew. He's the one I want—" Her bright-red cheeks shone like a beacon against her otherwise pale complexion. She checked herself before saying anything further.

"Marcus," snapped Martha as she swatted at him with her kitchen towel, "leave the child alone. You should be ashamed meddling in someone else's business that way."

He sat upright and moved to the edge of his chair, his tone incensed. "Why, I'm just as responsible for Jane and Mary as I am the twins. If young Wade needs a prod, then I'm the one that should do it."

Mary only partially listened to all that was said. Her lack of sleep and Josh's absence wore on her. Finally, she spoke, "I think," they all stopped speaking and turned to her. "He's waiting for Josh to return. Matt wants to ask his permission to marry Jane."

Everyone in the room continued to stare at her. "What makes you think that, Dear," asked Martha?

Mary smiled. "It's mostly a feeling, but every time I run into him, he asks if I've heard anything from Josh and when is he due back. Each time I tell him the same thing—I haven't heard anything for months. He says, 'If you hear anything, please let me know'." She reached to pat Jane's hand. "You're Matt's choice. When Josh returns maybe it'll be a double wedding."

To change the subject, Martha said, "Dinner's ready."

Martha served roasted chicken, cooked vegetables, and fresh-baked bread; pie for dessert. It was an enjoyable evening. Martha never seemed to tire of having her house abuzz with the children and their activities. She smiled as she watched Jane and twins laughed at Marcus' stories. She stared at Mary. "You know he'll be back soon, dear—you shouldn't worry so."

Mary smiled. "I know, Martha, it's just that—." She paused. "I guess I'm just tired is all. A good night's sleep is what I need."

After dessert, which she only tasted, Mary excused herself and returned to the bungalow, alone. The visit with Martha and Marcus brought a pleasant break from the loneliness she felt since Duncan's departure. He promised to return for her, but beyond two letters received shortly after his departure, she heard nothing more. Her confidence in Duncan as a capable man, who has, on more than one occasion, and in her presence, shown his abilities provided her some comfort. She knew he was alive; she felt she would somehow know if he wasn't, but why hadn't he returned?

She stoked the fire in the stove and heated water for a hot cup of tea. The tea set had been one of Martha's. Its white porcelain background set off the tiny roses sprinkled about. She filled the pot with boiling water and retreated to the front porch of their craftsman style house. She guessed it was nearly one-hundred-years old. Thanks to the community's foresight, they'd not let in fall into disrepair.

Steeped, Mary poured a cup of tea and gazed at the stars. It was something she, and Josh, did often before he left. The darkness of the new moon made the night sky a perfect black background; the stars sparkled like diamonds on velvet. Maybe he was watching them, too. That thought gave her a warm rush of pleasure.

Lost in her thoughts, Mary didn't hear the door as it opened. A huge figure stepped through and stood behind her. Too late, she sensed a presence just as a large hand clamped across her mouth nearly shutting off her breathing. Another hand slid around her waist and lifted her as a child did a small doll. The only noise came from the fallen tea cup as it dropped and shattered on the porch.

Mary struggled against her captor with all her strength. Her eyes widen with the realization of her nightmare's fruition. She kicked and flailed her arms at the man-beast who held her, but to no avail. Aside from a soft grunt, the giant seemed not to notice her efforts of escape.

Off the porch and across the road in the night's shadows waited her captor's partner; smaller in stature, but still a large man. When the hand dropped from her mouth, she gasped a breath to scream; a wad of cloth stuffed in her mouth choked off her intent. A gag was tied to prevent her from expectorating the now saliva soaked cloth. Her survival skills took charge; she realized she needed to take care and not swallow. The cud of cloth might lodge in her throat, and she would choke to death.

Her hands bound behind her back, the man-beast tossed her across a saddle effortlessly and tied her to prevent her falling off. Slowly, the three of them rode eastward out of New Lovelock. A single thought flashed in her mind; The Leader survived!

Away from New Lovelock, her captors removed the gag and allowed her to expel the wad of cloth. She took several deep breaths, and moisture returned to her mouth. She considered screaming; someone might hear. Afraid they would gag her again; she held her voice. Instead, she asked, "Why have you kidnapped me—where are you taking me?" Neither of the men responded. She steeled herself and asked the question she already knew the answer to, "Is the Leader still alive?" She waited, but they gave no reply.

Astride her mount, Mary studied her captors.

Like the Leader, they were clothed in black. Their faces were shadowed by the brims of their hats, but she could see they wore beards. The larger of the two reminded Mary of some great beast; his head seemed stuck on massive shoulders and when he looked at her, his whole body turned. He grinned at her. His lips spread across his face not with happiness, but rather with a leer of evil intent. "God healed the Leader, and now he'll have his prophesied bride—at least the first one."

Visibly shaken, Mary drew back from his words. The man-beast confirmed the Leader lived and still intended to wed Mary and her sisters. She trembled as the image of Kimball reaching out to touch her flashed in her mind. The thought of him with her sisters caused bile to rise. She fought it down and rode on in silence.

They rode through the night and into the early-morning hours, Mary found herself exhausted. She'd not been on a horse since arriving to New Lovelock. This many hours riding without a break rubbed the skin on her legs raw and the cramp in her muscles left her sore and stiff. The men showed no signs of stopping soon.

The morning light broke above the far

mountains. Across the tall grasses covering the rolling hills, wild flowers strained to face the sun absorbing its life-giving energy. For just an instant, she could ignore her discomfort and enjoy the sunrise. Then a stabbing pain in her leg returned her to her plight which; she thought bitterly, contracted the beauty of the day's beginning.

Rubbing the cramp from her leg, she glanced at her captures. At least now, she could see more clearly what they looked like. They dressed in black, the style of Kimball's personal guard. She didn't recall seeing either of them before, so they must be new to Henefer.

Their behavior made her suspect of their belief that Kimball is God's prophet; a belief held by Kimball's former guards. They were killed during an earlier attempted kidnapping of Mary and her sisters. Kimball and his guard took them in the night, but Josh, and Lucky, his wolf companion, rescued them. The Leader escaped, but since not even Lucky could find his remains, it was assumed he'd drown in the river where his scent ended.

She glanced at the morning sun now above the mountains. At home, it was time for Jane and her to start their day. Jane would go to Mary's room when she didn't appear in the kitchen for their morning tea. What would she think? There were no indications of a struggle … but there's the broken cup on the porch. Would Jane find it and get suspicious? No, not until she got to work and found that no one had seen her. Only then would she go to Marcus Atkins and the militia. They'd search the town before pursuing other options. Would they suspect that Kimball still lived and made good his promise to capture Mary and had plans for her sisters, too?

The militia's search would be slow. They couldn't afford to chase blindly after her when they didn't know the circumstances of her abduction. If they could figure that out in time, there was a chance they might catch up and save her. How could she signal Matt Wade, and the militia? She thought about her options, which were limited; and then slowly, a plan came to her. She would need them to stop.

"Please I need to stop," she said and looked at the larger man; her eyes pleading. "I have to pee."

"Hold up, William," said the larger man. "I could use a break, too." After he tied the lead for Mary's horse to his saddle horn, he dismounted. With his hand sliding along the rope, he walked back to Mary's horse. In a quick sequence, he untied her legs from the saddle's stirrups, swept her out of the saddle, and placed her on the ground.

Mary turned around and presented her hands; he hesitated. "I have to have my hands free—"

"She's got you there, John," said William. Mary looked back and saw William grin as he gibed his partner.

John uttered a noise that sounded akin to a bear's growl. William laughed; quick-witted responses, it seemed, were not John's strong suit. Perturbed, John untied Mary's hands and gave her a shove. "Over there in that group of bushes—" He pointed toward an outcropping with an isolated clump of shrubs. It would provide her privacy, but nothing more. "Mind that we can see if you try to run."

Concealed behind the bushes, Mary acted on her plan. Wearing cotton pants and a long-sleeve shirt with sleeves turn up and held with safety pins, she removed a pin from her shirt. From her pocket, she pulled a white handkerchief. She carefully spread it on the rock before her. Using the pin, she pricked the side of her hand several times until it began to bleed. With the looped end of the pin, she collected blood to use as ink. In a crude fashion, she printed: 'Kimball is alive-Mary'.

She hadn't lied to John; she really did have to pee, so while the note dried, she took care of that while she had the privacy. As she reassembled herself, she considered the note. If she merely let it fall, it could easily blow away never to be found. Near the bushes, she spied a small stone, she picked it up and tied the cloth around it and stuffed it in her rear pocket.

Ready, she stood and stepped away from the bushes and returned to the road. John waited, as she suspected, with cords to tie her hand. As she turned and presented her hands, she asked, "Is this really necessary. You've got my horse's lead, so I'd be on foot—"

John looked to William, who shrugged. "She's got a point, John. If she tries anything, we can tie her then." This time, John shrugged and walked Mary to her horse and unceremoniously tossed her into the saddle. By the time she recovered from the manhandling, John was mounted and leading her horse.

Standing in the stirrups, she rubbed her backside and secreted the message from her pocket. As they rode passed several potholes, she dropped the weighted note into a hole. She lifted her eyes and whispered, "Please, God, don't let it rain."

Chapter 3

When Jane returned from dinner at the Atkins', the house was dark and silent, so she quietly let herself in; not wanting to wake her sister. For weeks, Mary hasn't slept. She told Jane about the recurring nightmare she had night-after-night. 'It's always the same,' said Mary. 'I'm alone in a dark room, and I can sense movement in the shadows. There is a stream of light, like from a hole in the wall, and suddenly the Leader's face appears. His black eyes are crazed; he reaches out to grab me. I can't move or fight back— then I wake up cold and clammy.'

In the dark, Jane made ready for sleep. Martha Atkins made all the girls sleeping gowns. The light-blue flannel shift felt cool next to her skin, but soon, she'd be warm and snuggled under the covers. In the quiet of the night alone with her thoughts, the images created by Mary's telling of her dream filled her mind.

They were of Kimball, his stringy black hair flutter in an unfelt breeze, his eyes red with fury, and long sinewy fingers wiggled like snakes as he reached to snatch her. Her sleep was fitful and when morning came, she remained fatigued from nightmares of her own.

Jane was first into the kitchen. When she went to the stove to start a fire, she found that the kindling for the stove's firebox wasn't set. That's odd she thought; Mary usually did that chore before going to bed; but then Mary's been so tired lately. Jane glanced at Mary's bedroom door. She was not sure why, but a feeling of grave concern came over her. She stood in the center of the kitchen and turned slowly in a circle. Jane closely examined her surroundings. Something was wrong; she could sense it. On second thought, she supposed it was a carryover from her nightmares. She gave a shiver and returned to cooking breakfast.

As she moved about the kitchen performing her morning chores, Jane clanked the pots and pans and clanged the dishes as she set the table, but still no sound from Mary's room. When the coffee boiled, Jane sighed and called, "Alright sleepyhead it's time to get out of bed." She paused, but heard nothing, so, she went to Mary's bedroom door and knocked. "Mary, it's time to get up. Mary, are you awake?" Jane opened the door ….

***

"You say that's the way you found her room," asked Atkins?

"Yes, Uncle Marcus, her bed has not been slept in. When I searched the house I didn't see any sign of a struggle."

"Out here, Colonel," called Captain Matt Wade, Atkins' aid. Wade, a tall slender young man with sandy-brown hair and very blue eyes courted Jane Evans with the intention of marriage. Atkins and Jane came out onto the porch. They saw Wade kneeling in the yard; he traced his fingertips over the marks in the grass. "There's a broken cup on the porch. Down here are tracks—three horses waited for a long while—see where they moved about. Footprints lead from the house to the horses, only one set, but they're deep. He must've carried her."

Wade and Atkins looked at Jane, who'd left the porch to see the prints. She stood with trembling hands to her mouth, her face paled, and her pale-blue eyes spilled streams down her cheeks. "It's The Leader," she said.

Matt rose and took her into his arms and stroked the back of her neck. She sobbed on his shoulder. To console her, Wade said, "Kimball's dead, Jane."

"—but they never found his body," said Jane. "You don't know him like we do. He's evil, and he seems to defy the laws of nature. It's like he's not really human."

"Matt," interrupted Marcus, "get a detail of men together while these tracks are fresh. Put two of your best scouts to follow the tracks, and the rest of you ride east—" He paused and stared at Jane. Without looking away, he added, "Just in case Jane is right about Kimball."

"How long of a head start do they have," asked Wade?

"Assume they took her right after she left my place—" His brow lifted as he stared at nothing while he did the calculations. "They have a twelve-hour lead. My guess is they will have ridden all night to increase their advantage." Wade nodded and moved to leave. "Wade—" The captain halted. "Tell each man to take two horses, and rations for a week." With a nod, Wade left at a run.

A short while later; following the trackers, Wade led his horse to where Jane waited by her front porch. She still appeared upset. "Don't worry, Jane, we'll catch them."

She folded herself into his arms and nuzzled his neck. In a quiet voice, she said, "Please promise me you'll be careful, Matt. The Leader's guards are dangerous."

With his horse between them and his men, Wade lowered his face to hers. She returned his kiss passionately. His face was flushed and his voice husky, he said, "I'll be back—"

Chapter 4

It was dusk, Mary and her abductors rode non-stop for almost twenty hours. She was exhausted, so were their horses. Her lower back throbbed, and her chafed backside felt tender when she rubbed it seeking relief. She glanced at the lathered animals; they wheezed and thrust their heads forward with each stride. If they didn't stop soon the animals would collapse. Mary experienced mixed emotions. If the horses couldn't go further, then they would be on foot and easier to catch. On the other hand, she didn't wish to see the horses maimed.

Events soon took the dilemma out of her hands when they turned up a paved side road. They halted after a few yards; William dismounted, and he walked back to the main road. Several minutes later, he returned. "We're clear—there's no trace we left the main road." He chuckled at their cleverness. "By the time they think to double back to this road, we'll be half way to Henefer."

Mary considered jumping from her horse, and racing back to the main road to trample weeds or do something to leave a sign. In the end, she decided to wait for a better chance of escape.

A half-hour further on, they turned off again. This time it was a gravel road that led to an abandoned farm. The house and outbuildings stood empty for decades. Rot left holes in the roofs; there was no longer any sign of what the roofing materials had been. The structures sagged barely able to remain erect. Surly the next wind storm would topple them. Inside the farm's animal pen, with its missing rails crudely replaced with recently cut tree branches, waited six fresh mounts.

The horses piqued Mary's interest. Most likely, they staged the horses here for later use; she thought. Could someone else be around? She again looked at the horses. They'd planned on kidnapping Jane and the twin also; she smiled ruefully. William watched, and as if he read her mind, he said, "We left them here five days ago. We ain't going straight east to Henefer." His smile transformed into a sneer. "We're going to travel north through Boise and then down to Henefer. Even if your friends do figure it out—it'll be too late to save you."

Each word William spoke stung as it cut deeper; killing her hope of rescue. Her shoulders slumped with resignation; how would Josh ever find her now?

John lifted her off her horse and led the way to a shelter they'd built from remnants of the battered old farm house. They made a cold camp that night. After they ate, she sought her bedroll and despite her anxiety, Mary slept like the dead. On the trail thereafter, she remained sluggish. Exhaustion and despair took their toll; soon time passed without notice.

The days began to blurred one into the next. They rode, ate, and slept. When they neared a compound, the only place, Mary could hope to find help, they gagged her and in the night, they skirted those communities unseen. Mary realized that even if Colonel Atkins crossed their trail, he would find no confirmation they'd passed. Finally, her despair and depression were complete. Despondency took hold, and she became listless and tractable. She stood until told to sit, ate when given food, and slept at their commands; she showed no signs of self-will. Eventually, they felt no need to restrain her.

Avoiding travelers, few as there were, and averting compounds made their travel time to Henefer a greater duration than necessary. Day-after-day of seeing the same tree-lined road, soon, Mary lost sense of time, but she knew weeks had passed.

It was mid-morning when they arrived at the gates of Henefer. Its twenty-foot walls were constructed of masonry blocks and timbers harvested from the nearby forest. The gates, which were over twelve-foot high, were made from hand-hewn yellow pine and swung from heavy iron strap hinges; four on each gate. A single four-foot by eight-foot tall sally port cut into the right-hand gate opened when they arrived. An armed guard stepped out to greet them. "Welcome home, Brothers," said the guard.

Mary's clothes were dirty and tattered; since her capture, she'd had no personal time, or privacy to bathe. As they rode through the compound, Mary heard one of the women say, "The poor thing, she's obviously in shock. I hope they hung those kidnappers."

Another spoke, "What's happened to her three sisters?" Several women drifted toward the compound gates as if expecting more riders with

Mary's sisters. When none appeared, they turned back to Mary and followed her to the Leader's internal compound; a group of five houses surrounded by a patrolled fence. The community did not resent the fence; they felt it provided more protection to them than their leader.

They dismounted outside the perimeter. William left with the horses. "I'll see to the animals, you deal with him." John nodded and pushed Mary forward through the wrought iron gates.

Mary glanced at the gate's guard. He was young, not much older than she; there was concern in his eyes. Could he, or anyone, help her now? She stopped and scanned the people beyond the gate. All she saw in their eyes, before they looked away, or cast stares downward, was fear.

John clamped his beefy right hand around Mary's upper arm and forcibly walked her toward the Leader's house; a two-story limestone mansion. It was flanked by smaller houses similarly constructed for his existing wives and children. They, like most who had intimate knowledge of Kimball, strove to stay out of his path and thoughts. His cruelty knew no bounds, especially with his children. Sired by a man who was the product of generations of incest, their gene pool was shallow. However, though they weren't intelligent, they were all as cunning and ruthless as any wild animal; rumors spread of his sons about their torture of pets. When they were outside their enclave, the community guarded their daughters.

Inside the mansion, a word from John to one of the guards sent him rushing up the center staircase. John and Mary waited. She felt his approach before she actually saw him bounding down the staircase. When she saw him, she drew her fist into her mouth and bit hard to keep from screaming in horror.

Though she wanted to, she couldn't force herself to look away. She stared; he looked worse than anything she had imagined in her nightmares. Kimball's black mane flew back from his face as he rushed at her. An unseeing white orb remained of his right eye. The raised scars where Lucky tore at his face were pink with streaks of white. They'd healed on their own without attention. He waved his arms, rather his right arm; the left was gone below the elbow. His physique appeared as a mere hollow shell of his once sinewy self. His features where sunken and his clothes hung from his lanky form. As he did in her dreams, he appeared as a fiend, but more so. He seemed the archetype of all evil. When he reached out and touched her, she whimpered as if struck, and then fainted.

When Mary opened her eyes, she saw that two women attended her, whom after a few minutes of staring she recognized as Judith and Sharon Kimball, the Leader's two youngest wives. Sharon, Kimball's newest wife, blonde and blue-eyed like Mary, turned to her and said, "Lie still, Mary. You're exhausted and need to rest and take nourishment."

Judith, a slightly older version of Sharon, approached. "We'll start with this chicken broth." While Sharon lifted Mary's head, Judith spooned several bites to Mary's lips. Mary shook her head, and Sharon lowered it back to the pillow.

"Thank you," said Mary, "but I'm not that hungry—water."

From a pitcher setting on nightstand near the bed, Sharon poured a glass and raised Mary's head. Mary took the glass. "Thank you, I can manage." She used both hands to hold the glass and drank the entire glass in four gulps. She lay back and gave them a weak smile. Searching their eyes, Mary saw compassion. It gave her hope, and she asked, "What is to happen to me?"

Sharon and Judith exchanged glances. "We told him you were in shock and would need time to recover," said Judith. "He has instructed us to see to your needs, and nurse you back to health." As Judith spoke, she and Sharon cast their eyes down to avoid making eye contact with Mary. "We can't delay him for long, but you can expect a week to strengthen yourself and prepare for what's ahead."

Strange she thought; I don't feel afraid—angry yes, but there is no fear. Was she that confident that Josh would save her? Or, was it that she was no longer the frightened child who fled The Leader so many months ago. Now that her nightmare had come to fruition, she had to face Kimball, he didn't terrify her.

She looked at the two women; the earlier few spoons of broth provided more strength than Mary at first realized. She said, "I'll have the soup now, please." Sharon smiled turned and retrieved the bowl.

As Sharon presented it, she said, "It's not hot— do you want it warmed, or a fresh bowl?"

Mary struggled to push herself up in the bed and leaned against the bed's brass headboard. She reached out for the bowl. "No, its fine, I'll sip it from the bowl."

Over the next two-days, Mary's routine didn't vary. She slept, woke for water, or the toilet, and ate broth and softened foods. Early on the morning of the third-day, Mary came awake rested and hungry. She left the bed and sat at the dressing table across the room. Morning sun shone bright through the room's window onto the mirror and lit her face. Color had returned to her cheeks and the dark circles that ringed her eyes were gone. She felt more like herself than she had since her abduction from New Lovelock.

Sharon came in and Mary smiled at her, she said, "I'd like something more substantial than broth for breakfast—is that possible?" Sharon smiled back, nodded, and left the bedroom.

When Sharon returned, she carried a tray of food. She sat it on the table by the bed; oatmeal, fruit, and bread. Judith also came in and sat with Sharon. As Mary ate she studied the two women, they could be her cousins. Sharon, twenty, married the Leader when she was fifteen. Judith, twenty-five, also married the Leader when she was fifteen. It was a pattern; the Leader preferred young brides. When they neared twenty, he tired of them. Mary asked, "Is there five-years between all of Kimball's wives?"

Judith stared hard at Mary. Finally, she said, "You've noticed." Her accompanying laugh held no humor. "He likes us young and obedient. When we turn twenty or have children, he finds a new wife. You and his sisters were to hold him for a spell—"

"Why did you agree to marry him?" asked Mary.

Sharon spoke, "We were only fifteen. He wasn't as bad then—" She paused to wipe a tear. "Our parent wanted it too, so—" She shrugged her shoulders and looked at Mary her eyes were filled with sadness.

"It's after he became obsessed with you and your sisters—that's when he began to change." Judith's tone was harsh.

Mary drew back. "You blame us?"

Judith stood and walked to the door. She paused at the door and without looking back, she said, "It was a peaceful life; he's not bothered me since he married Sharon." As she spoke, her voice was monotone and listless. She rushed out.

"She doesn't mean that," said Sharon. "He changed before then—" Sharon absently stroked her left arm comforting herself as she continued. "I saw it when I came; I think even my parents suspected something wasn't right, but—" Again; she left the obvious unsaid, but the unspoken words filled the room.

"I know," interrupted Mary, "if you defy the Leader, you and your family will suffer. I think he had my parents killed." She paused and put her hands to her face and stared down. "I've never admitted that before." A tinge of anger grew in her voice.

Chapter 5

Duncan rode from San Francisco to New Lovelock in eighteen-days. The arduous journey tested the mettle of Duncan's patience, and the endurance of his animals. Though exhausted, he kept their halts short. He only allowed scarcely enough time for minimal rest and to feed his animals, and then he returned to the saddle.

Though, he sensed they were nearby, or at least hoped they were, he hadn't seen Lucky, or his mate Shadow over the last day-four. Had his friend and trail companion left to begin a new life without him?

The lights were still on at the Atkins' house when Duncan rode up. Weary and filthy, he dragged his feet as he climbed the porch steps. Martha opened the door before he knocked. "Josh, you poor thing, get in here and set yourself down." She grabbed his arm and tugged him into her kitchen. "There's fresh coffee—"

Comfortably planted in a chair at her kitchen table, he smiled as she sat a cup in front of him. He hadn't had a good cup of coffee since he left San Francisco. Suddenly, exhaustion awash him, and he didn't seem to have the strength to lift the cup. Seconds passed, then the aroma of the brew floated to his nostrils and just as quickly, nothing could have prevented him from drinking the hot dark rich tasting brew.

Duncan lingered over his cup letting the moisture from its steam soften his face. When Marcus Atkins entered the kitchen, he took one look at Duncan and without a word of greeting disappeared and returned from his den with his bottle of whiskey. "Son you need a healthy jigger of this to bolster you up. You look terrible—did you even stop to rest?" Ordinarily, Martha protested her husband's consumption of alcohol in the house, but this time she withheld her objections.

"I take it that you've received Matt's message?" continued Marcus, as he took a seat next to Duncan.

"Marcus," snapped Martha. "Leave him be until after I get some food into him, and he's had a chance to sleep."

Duncan raised his hand to quell her words.

"Martha, it's all right. I need to know what's happened, and then I can sleep."

Martha glared at Marcus as if somehow it was his fault Duncan didn't wished to be mothered. She turned back to the stove. "If that's what you want.

Marcus said, "Let me get someone to see to your animals." He rose to go outside, and then stepped back. "Is that wolf still with you? The whiskey revived Duncan; humor shown in pale green his eyes, he grinned at Marcus. "He's my best friend on the trail and most other places, too, but I'm sad to say he's found a mate, and I've not seen much of him them for two-weeks—not at all for the last four days."

Duncan walked outside with Marcus. One of his militia stood nearby and he ordered him to see to Buck and the girl's needs. Duncan watched as they vanished in the night, but he did not return to the kitchen. Instead, he moved to the end of the porch and sat in one of the two rockers nestled with a table for drinks. "Marcus, I need to know everything that happened."

Marcus heaved a great sigh and dropped into the rocker next to Duncan. "Son, there's not a lot to tell. Mary and Jane came over to our place for dinner. Mary left early—said she was tired. Jane told us later that Mary had been having nightmares about Kimball still bein' alive."

"Kimball!" Duncan stood and began to pace the length of the porch. His fingers opened and closed as he struggled to make sense from what Marcus said. He stopped and stared at his friend; doubt clouded his eyes. "I just don't see how that's possible. No one could have survived—Lucky couldn't find a trace. If he had survived—"

"That's what we figured too, but—" Marcus carefully removed a folded piece of cloth from his shirt pocket. "We found this on the road east." He handed it to Duncan.

Duncan read the words, 'Kimball is alive. Mary'. He looked up at Marcus and then back to the cloth. Holding it nearer the light from the doorway, he squinted to see better, and asked, "Is this blood, her blood?" His jaw tightened as he looked off into the night. "If they've harmed her, I'll—" He didn't finish.

Marcus shrugged as his reply. Then added, "That's the only thing we found and there no signs of her being hurt. They wouldn't have gone to all this trouble just to hurt her." Marcus paused then changed the subject. "Wade and his men rode to Salt Lake, but didn't find anything. If Kimball's got here at his compound, there's not much chance of gettin' her back."

"I don't accept that, Marcus." Duncan dropped into the rocker "Mary means everything to me—I shouldn't have left, but—"

"Had you been here, Duncan, they might have killed you in your sleep. The fault is mine. You said we should have killed Kimball and his men while they slept. I just couldn't believe anyone could be that evil—I'm sorry I didn't listen to you, Duncan."

Duncan saw the pain on Marcus' face and heard the sincere regret in his voice. A sigh passed Duncan's lips as he reached out to grip the older man's arm. "You wouldn't be the man you are if you'd done what I suggested. You're a moral man, Marcus—a good friend, too."

Marcus didn't respond. Their silence was broken by Martha. "There you two are—come in here. I've hot food for Duncan."

Duncan pushed himself out of the rocker. Marcus said, "You go on in. I'll check on your animals— then; I'll be along."

Martha opened the screen door and pulled at Duncan's shirt sleeve. "Come along, you need food and rest. While you eat, I'll prepare a hot bath. After, you can get some rest and we'll figure things out tomorrow."

Duncan followed Martha into her kitchen and sat down before what looked like a feast compared to the last three weeks on the trail. He carefully folded the blood stained piece of cloth and put it in his shirt pocket. As Martha fussed about the stove, he bowed his head over interlocked fingers and prayed for the first time in his life.

The hearty meal and hot bath accomplished what Martha hoped, Duncan slept like the dead until nearly 8:00. When he awoke, he followed the smell of coffee to the kitchen. Martha heard him stirring and waited with a cup of the dark brew. "It's fresh," she said. "Sit down and I'll fix you something to eat."

The twins tumbled into the kitchen from outside. Still all arms and legs, but showing the budding signs of becoming young women. Their face radiated their indomitable spirts. Helen said, "Finally, you're up!"

Sarah chimed in, "We thought you'd never wake up, sleepy-head."

They threw themselves about his neck and squeezed. Coughing, Duncan pulled at their arms. "You're choking me, Girls."

They released him, but didn't move away. Each

kept a hand on his shoulder as if to insure he wouldn't leave. "Sorry," they said in unison. He gave them a reassuring smile and put an arm around each and hugged them back. "When will you get Mary back, Duncan? She's been gone for weeks now."

"Girls let him eat," said Martha as she placed a plate of food in front of him. "There's plenty more when that's gone."

Duncan scanned the plate of food. "I'm sure this'll be more than enough." Four cups of coffee and a second plate of food later, he pushed back from the table. "I'm embarrassed to have eaten so much, Martha, but you're an awfully good cook."

"Thank you, Duncan. It pleases me that you think so."

The twins looked up from the watching Duncan eat when Jane came through the door followed my Matt Wade. "Josh—" She began to weep. "Kimball's got Mary. I let her go home alone, and they grabbed her. I didn't realize it until that next morning."

Duncan stood and Jane rushed into his arms. "Marcus told me everything. There's nothing you could have done. Had you been there they'd have taken you too." He took a deep cleansing breath. "I'll get her back, Jane, don't you or the twins worry."

Matt held back and waited for Jane to compose herself. When she released Duncan, he moved forward and offered his hand. "I want to go with you, Duncan, if you'll have me."

"Thank you, Matt. I need all the help I can get." Duncan's demeanor changed. He ignored Martha and the girls as he walked towards the door. Duncan was on the hunt, and nothing else mattered right now but Mary. "Is it possible to have a rider take several mounts and carry a message to Wyoming"?

"I believe so, but the commander will have to give the order," said Matt. Duncan and Wade made their way to Atkins' command post.

The post consisted of three buildings constructed from timber logs. The center building was its operational command, where Marcus' office was located. To the north stood the barracks and forming a semi-circle to the south were the supply and armory buildings. In front of the command building, inside a ring of painted white stones sat a piece of WWII vintage artillery appropriated from the VFW. They'd also salvaged from the VFW, a forty-foot flag pole which flew the flag of the United States.

Matt led Duncan inside. From behind his desk, Marcus rose to greet them. "You look much better this morning, Josh. You were pretty much all-in last night." He smiled. "Goes to show what Martha's cooking and some rest will do for you."

"Yes, I needed rest and nourishment, thank you, Marcus." Duncan scanned Marcus' office. Nothing changed since his last visit. It was the same nondescript building with Spartan furnishings. He moved to the small table that served as Marcus' conference table; it seated six.

As they settled in, Marcus asked, "Coffee—it's fresh?"

Duncan nodded. Matt stood. "I'll get it, Sir.

Matt moved to the potbellied stove. When it's warm, like the present, a small fire burned to boil coffee and water for herb teas. In the winter, the stove glowed red and the conference table moved closer. With three-mugs looped over the fingers of his left hand and the coffee pot in his right; Matt came to the table and set out the cups. Marcus and Duncan began to talk. "What's on your mind, Josh?"

Duncan waited for and sipped his coffee before he answered. "Marcus, I need to dispatch riders with spare horse to ride non-stop. One rider goes to Green River, Wyoming and the other north of there to the state prison."

Marcus studied Duncan's face for several seconds before he responded. "I guess that's possible, but what's there that we can't provide from here?"

"Men who will set aside their morals and do what's needed to get Mary back," said Duncan. His eyes were cold as steel, and his voice filled with the iron of his conviction. He added,"—and who will do what's need to make sure it's ended."

The militia commander leaned back in his chair his shoulders slumped, and his eyes stared. Duncan could see their sadness. "I know I refused to murder Kimball when we had the chance, but—"

"No, Marcus, it's not that—" Duncan's voice softened; it became less harsh as he continued, "I've fought side-by-side with the men I'm talking about; I know they can do what's needed and live with the consequences. I don't wish to put that burden on you or anyone else."

His words hung unanswered for several seconds, and then Marcus sighed and placed his hands flat on the table in surrender. "As you wish, Son, but at least take a few men from here. They'll have to be volunteers and only after you've explained the danger."

"I'd like to go, Duncan," said Matt. "I feel like they've taken my sister." There was a hint of a smile on Duncan's face as he glanced up at the young captain. "What's Jane going to think about you doing this?"

Matt stiffened; his jaw clenched. "What would she think if I didn't?"

Duncan's stare hardened. "It'll be tough, and there'll be killings you'll have to live with—can you do that?"

"Kimball still wants Jane and the twins. If killing him and some of his men will prevent that, then I'm in."

Duncan pushed up from the table. "All right, I'll take volunteers from New Lovelock. Matt, you gather the men who you think we can use and meet me back here in an hour." He glanced at Marcus. "Is that alright with you?" The commander nodded.

Captain Wade marched from the office. Duncan asked, "Now, can we talk about those dispatch riders?"

By the time Wade returned, Duncan had completed his dispatches. Marcus gave one to each rider with specific instructions about their delivery. He returned to his office and found the men, all dressed in their khakis, milling about waiting. "Gentlemen, I assume you've some idea of what this is about, so I'll get to the point. This is strictly a volunteer mission. It does not have a direct connection to New Lovelock save the Evans sisters. Mr. Duncan will be in command." Atkins scanned the faces of his men. They were to a man not yet twenty-one. "Some of you may not come back—think hard about volunteering for this mission. Duncan, I'll leave them to you. Please try to bring them all back alive."

Duncan scanned their faces. Including Wade, there were fifteen men; Wade being the oldest. They drilled, and they were fit; Duncan was sure each man was an expert marksman, but could they kill another human being; even to save their own lives, or the life of a comrade? Some of them, if not all, were barely old enough to shave. He rubbed his own jaw and thought; the same could be said about him. This last year had matured and hardened him; something he didn't wish for them. Did he really want to be responsible for so many lives? The circumstances gave him no other choice if he was to save Mary.

He sighed. "Gentlemen, your attention please," said Duncan. The room quieted and all eyes were on him. "Colonel Atkins is correct. This mission has nothing to do with New Lovelock, and everything to do New Lovelock. You live in an open community much as they did before the Decline. Can New Lovelock afford to become known as a town where men with desires for young women can enter at will and steal one?" Duncan waited for the mumbling to settle and then continued, "Mary Evans has been kidnapped from her home by John Kimball also known as The Leader. Some of you were involved eight-months ago when Kimball kidnapped Mary and her three sisters; nearly killing Colonel Atkins."

"We thought he was dead," said one of the men.

"So did I," said Duncan. He paused to fish from his pocket the piece of rag with Mary's words. "This note from Mary, written using her blood as ink, says Kimball is alive."

Once again, the room came alive with murmurs as the men talked to one another. One spoke out, "What's the plan, Duncan?"

That was the question Duncan couldn't answer—yet. "I haven't worked out all the details, but—" He glanced at the wall mounted pre-decline road map of the United States. As he moved to the wall, they gathered around. He stabbed his finger at New Lovelock. "We leave at first light and travel from here," he dragged his finger across the map, "to here southeast of Salt Lake City. I've sent dispatches to friends in Wyoming who will be waiting for us."

"How many men," asked Wade?

"I hope another half dozen. We'll camp outside Henefer staying out of sight and study their compound. The plan is to infiltrate the compound, locate and rescue Mary, and kill Kimball." Several of the men looked startled. Duncan's jaw clenched as he stared back. "Gentlemen, let me be more precise; we will assassinate John Kimball." He scanned their faces for several seconds letting his words settle in their minds. "Anyone who isn't prepared to commit cold blooded murder should not go."

A couple of the young men swallowed hard, but none looked away. Wade said, "We understand."

Duncan nodded. "First light then—I won't think ill of anyone who changes their mind, and I hope nor will anyone else here."

Chapter 6

When the service finished, they escorted Mary back to her room. Judith and Sharon were there to help her change into her nightclothes. "This really isn't necessary, I'm fully recovered," said Mary, she hoped they would leave her alone.

"The Leader says we are to see to your every need," said Sharon. She gave Mary a weak smile. "So long as he thinks you need us, he'll leave you be."

Judith stood with her arms crossed and scowled at Mary, her eyes reproachful. "We can leave and tell Leader you're fully recovered if that's what you want."

Mary's eyes widened. Her panic was plain and confirmed by the quiver in her voice. "No, please don't—"

A bitter mocking laugh issued from Judith. "Why should we risk his wrath for your sake? No one helped us when we came."

"That's not true, Judith," said Sharon. "When I arrived you were so grateful that someone else was taking your place, you told me you felt guilty. You knew the abuse I was going to be subjected to—you cried. Surely, you can't have forgotten?"

Judith's gaze fixed on the window with her arms wrapped across her breast comforting herself; she did not respond. They stared at her and waited. A full minute passed, and then Judith spoke, "I do remember. I feel that same guilt now, but what can I do—nothing; there is nothing you or I can do."

Mary's eyes darted to the bedroom door, and then the second-floor window. She stepped closer to wives. "You could help me escape—"

Her words hung in the air; Judith and Sharon stared at Mary as if she had two-heads. The concept of leaving Henefer was so foreign to them that the thought had never entered their minds.

"What?" asked Sharon, as if she'd misheard Mary's words. "What did you just say?"

"Please keep your voices down," said Mary. "I said you could help me escape from the compound. Once I'm beyond the gates, I can get away on my own." Mary's jaw tightened. "I've done it before."

Sharon glanced at Judith and then back to Mary as she spoke, "We aren't allowed to leave the enclave. How would we ever help you to escape the compound?" Sharon's eyes widen with fear. As she spoke, she rubbed her hands nervously as if drying them. "If Leader ever found out—I don't know what he'd do, but it would be terrible." She shrank back and dropped into a chair.

Undeterred, Mary pressed. "Alright then, help me get out of the enclave, and I'll get out of the compound on my own." She looked to each in turn her eyes welled. "Please help me?"

Judith spoke first. "There is a way out. I used it a few times to sneak out and visit my parents after Sharon came. Leader and his people were focused on her, so it was easy."

"How," asked Mary? Lunging to her feet, she knocked Sharon, who also attempted to stand, back into her chair. Mary reached out and grabbed Judith's hand and squeezed. "Please tell how you got away."

Sharon stood and closed on Judith, too. "Well?" she asked."

The elder wife stepped back willing Mary and Sharon to give her space. "Are you afraid of heights, and can you climb?"

"No," said Mary, "and I can climb like a monkey—now tell me!"

A sigh escaped as Judith sat on the bench at the foot of the bed. "My room, across the hall, it faces the enclave's wall. Between my room and that wall is an old oak tree." She paused to give them a second to picture the setting. "You can climb from my window across to a branch that overhangs the wall. You'll have to drop a few feet, but it's not far."

Sharon's brow pinched as her head tilted. "How'd you get back in if the limb is higher?"

Judith smiled. "My father brought me back and boosted me up to the branch. He gave me some men's clothes, so I wouldn't stand out with others in the community. I still have them, and I'm sure they'll fit you, if you want, Mary."

"Oh yes please—thank you so much, Judith. Mary stood and moved to the door, what is the best time to leave your room?"

Judith smiled at Mary; she couldn't help herself. Mary's excitement was contagious. "Not for hours yet; after ten when the compound has settled in and few people are about. Where did you leave when you escaped the first time?"

Mary's eyes twinkled and her smile was gay and

impish. "Behind the warehouse there are always wooden boxes stacked against the wall. It's a long drop, but I'll manage."

"We've old linens stored in this room, Mary," said Sharon. "We could spend the time making a rope. Then you could lower yourself safely."

"That's a good idea," agreed Mary. "We'll make two lengths, and early before the house is awake, you tie one to bed frame and lower it out my window." Mary stood and looked down at the front of the house. "There are tall bushes to help conceal it. Then Leader won't suspect you helped me."

Sharon and Judith exchanged glances. "We were worried about," said Judith. "If he finds out, he beat us."

The comment angered Mary. "Then why do you stay?"

"Our children," said Judith. "Then after a while, he doesn't bother us older wives, so we just stay out of the way—it easier that way. My son is six now, maybe later when he's old enough to understand, I might try then."

Sharon said, "My daughter is only two, but I'll leave before she hits puberty. I will not have that incestuous monster near her. His first wife's child is a girl—near twelve. Leader watches her and we all worry, but especially Ann, her mother."

"But you have positions in the community. If you spoke out, maybe the people would come together and do something."

Sharon's stare harden, she said. "Like your parents, Mary?"

Mary turned on Sharon; her focus on the younger wife intense. "Do you know for sure that Leader had my parents killed? Please tell me if you know anything at all." Mary followed Sharon's glance at Judith.

Both the women cast their eyes elsewhere. Judith said, "Like you, we have suspicions, but no proof. Even if we did, we'd never get away with sharing it with anyone."

Mary exhaled slowly and lowered her shoulders; she suddenly felt weak. "I understand," said Mary. In a tone that conveyed her bitter disappointment, she asked, "Where is the linen, we should get started?"

It was after ten when they finished. They'd braided two lengths of bed sheets into knotted ropes. The longer of the two, she took with her to Judith's room. In the room's darkness, Judith pointed out the route to take through the tree.

She changed into the men's clothing. The clothes hung from Mary's small frame, but they would do. Sharon took canned foods, a knife, and some bread from the kitchen. Mary hugged the two women; she slung the bag with her supplies over her neck and shoulder. Judith opened the bedroom window while Sharon went to the door and listened. Judith craned out of the window and seeing the way was clear helped Mary crawl through.

There was a limb above the window for a handhold. Mary had to hop about four-feet to the larger tree branch below it. Mary looked down at the distance. "You wanted to visit home badly."

Judith smiled. "They've trimmed the tree several times since then. It was about the same or a little less."

Mary glanced at Judith and wished she had the woman's long legs. "Well here I go—" Clutching the limb; she hopped out onto the larger branch. Looking back it no longer seemed so far. She held out her arm and Judith passed the rope.

The route to the wall was an easy climb. She laid on the branch that hung over the wall. Uncoiling the rope, she lowered an equal length down each side of the branch; that way, she could pull the rope after her and have it to down-climb the compound's wall behind the warehouse.

The way was clear; she gripped the rope with both hands; steeled herself and swung off the branch. Mary surprised herself with the ease at which she lowered herself hand-over-hand to the ground. She glanced up and saw Judith biting her knuckle. When she was safely on the ground, Mary waved at her. Judith took in a huge breath before she returned the gesture.

Mary pulled the rope and watched it collect at her feet. Then she coiled and slung it over her shoulder. One last wave to Judith and she slipped silently into the compound's shadows.

Little changed since she was here last, so staying in the shadows and making her way to the warehouse was not difficult. When she rounded the corner of the old metal building, she stopped cold. There were no boxes against the compound's outside wall. Instead, the boxes were stacked against the warehouse. Testing their weight, she found they were too large and heavy for her to move.

Her resolve didn't falter, nor did she consider returning to the Leader's enclave. Rather, she studied the problem. After a few minutes, she noticed the top of the vertical log wall was irregular with occasional gaps. She fashioned a big knot on the end of her rope and flung it towards the top. Her first try fell short. The second and the third went over the edge, but failed to snag in a gap. On her fourth toss, the rope slid between two logs perfectly.

Fortunately, they decided to knot the rope. Using her hands and feet, she began the ascent. The climb exhausted her, but when she reached the top and straddled the wall, she felt exhilarated when she saw that her freedom was at hand. Mary tugged, but the rope would not come free. She hesitated, and then saw another gap two logs away. She looped the rope back around through the second gap and lowered the rope. She turned taking one last look at Henefer. "God, please don't let them catch me." She slid over and climbed down the wall. Once on the ground, she bolted north; the opposite they'd expect her to go; she hoped.

Chapter 7

"From Duncan, you say," asked Morgan Hayes, the Green River compound's lawman? The young blonde rider nodded. "You look all in, Son. Step down from your horse and come into my office. There's coffee and something stronger if you want it."

He glanced at the stone building located in the center of the compound. The young man did as he was bid. "Thank you, Sir. Coffee will be fine, but I could use something to eat."

The tall lean lawman glanced up from the letter with dark penetrating eyes, eyes that have caused more than one man to think twice before bracing Morgan Hayes; his stare softened. "You go to the Dram House down the street. Tell them Morgan Hayes sent you. They're to give you whatever you want and send me the bill."

A big smile creased the young man's face and

his pale blue eyes twinkled. "You sure about that—I could eat a horse."

Morgan chuckled. "At your age, I'd expect nothing less. Would you do me a favor while you're there?" The young man nodded. "Please ask for Bernie Olsson. He's a big blonde Swede; you can't miss him—tell him I need to see him right away."

The young man turned and looked at his horses, which were as every bit done in as much as he. He glanced up the street toward the livery. "Come on, boys, I'll get you some feed too."

"You go on to the Dram House; I'll have someone see to your animals." The rider hesitated; clearly not personally taking care of his mount was not how he'd been trained. Morgan cast a stern look. "I said, 'go on', I don't like repeating myself."

The young man stood at attention and restrained the impulse to salute. "Yes Sir." And he smartly pivoted and marched off toward the Dram House with his message for Bernie Olsson.

Green River, a trading community, did a fair amount of business. Its main street crowed with people who busied themselves going from one building to the next. The Dram House was located in the center of the business area; two doors north of the general store. The dispatch rider hurried inside in search of Bernie Olsson and food.

From his desk, Morgan looked up when Bernie filled the doorway. "Whatcha need, Morg?"

Morgan grimaced and then sighed. "My name is Morgan, Bernie. How many times do I have to ask you not to call me Morg?"

"But we're friends, Morg. Friends have nicknames—it's a rule; I think."

Bernie's innocent smile got the better of Morgan, and he shook his head trying not to smile in return. "Friends also do what their friend request. So I'm asking you to please stop calling me Morg—can you do that?"

"I can do that, Morg," said Bernie Olsson with a grin. The giant of a man entered Morgan's office and sat across the desk from Morgan. The big Swede appeared hulking in the small office which contained Morgan's desk and two jail cells. The pre-decline Police Department was outside the present-day compound.

At six-four and near three-hundred pounds, the blue-eyed blonde was the strongest man in the compound. He was married to Lisa Gamble-Olsson, who controlled the gentle giant with a look and hands on her hips. "The kid said you wanted to see me, and that it was urgent—whatcha need?"

"Why do I bother?" Morgan shook his head and sighed. "Read this—it's from Duncan." With surprising speed for someone so large, Bernie snatched the paper from Morgan.

'Dear Morgan and Bernie,

I don't have time for niceties. My fiancée, Mary Evans, has been kidnapped by a zealot named John Kimball. His compound, Henefer, is located southeast of Salt Lake City. I need your help.

Come with as many men as you can gather, and meet me at Coalville, which is a ghost town ten-miles south of Henefer. The men should be of your caliber—men who can and will perform as needed for the future good of those who survive.

I've sent a similar note to Farmer at the prison, but please don't wait for him to arrive. He may well take a different route, or decide not to come.

Hope to see you at Coalville.

Duncan'

As Bernie looked up, a solemn expression settled across his face. "Did you know Duncan was gettin' married?"

Morgan's eyes narrowed. "How would I know

that? This is the first bit of news we've heard."

"Oh, that makes sense," said Bernie. "What do you suppose he meant by 'men of our caliber'?"

That was a fair question. Morgan considered for several seconds before answering. Finally, he said, "I think it means we may have to execute some people for the greater good of others."

Morgan watched the confused expression on Bernie's face change to understanding. Bernie asked, "Like when Farmer killed your brother—to keep the peace?"

The lawman's expression did not register concern or the slightest ill will over the comment. He only nodded and added, "That's what I assume.

"Morgan, I can be ready to leave in an hour."

"We'll leave in the morning. There are preparations needed: weapons, dynamite, and men—if we can find any who'll join us."

"After what Duncan did for our compound—why I bet we'll have to turn them away," said Bernie.

A wry smile crooked the corners of Morgan's lips, and sadness veiled his eyes. "People in general have a short memory. They're not warriors; they'd need time to work up to the idea of riding off to fight for a girl they've never met. Even for Duncan—"

Bernie scowled; his meaty paws on the edge of Morgan's desk. He rose to his full height. "You don't seem to think much of the folks here—you had me fooled." There was an edge to his voice and crimson burned colored his cheeks.

"Calm down, Bernie," said Morgan as he raised his hands, palm out, in surrender. "I like the people of Green River and think they're good honest folks with families to rear and lives to live. But, like I said, they're not accepting of the idea of fighting."

"Well I think you're wrong, Mr. Morgan Hayes," said Bernie, as he turned to leave.

Bernie paused inside the doorway, Morgan said, "I hope I'm wrong, too." As Bernie glanced over his shoulder and nodded, Morgan saw that irritating grin of his start to grow.

"Sure thing, Morg—" Bernie stepped through the door and made good his escape before Morgan could have the last word.

Two-hours later, Morgan and Bernie sat at Gamble's kitchen table meeting with the compound's council members. "Well, Gentlemen, that's all the information we have," said Morgan.

"We're leavin' in the mornin'," added Bernie, "who's comin' with us?" He looked from one man to the next, but no one spoke. Bernie glanced at Morgan and then back to the council. "I know you ain't cowards. I saw you fight when we were attacked, and the way you stood up to Blackburn took plenty of guts. It's Josh Duncan askin' for our help. He saved this compound—we owe him everything." The men looked away, but none would answer. "I, I just don't believe it—"

Morgan placed his hand on Bernie's shoulder. "Let's go, Bernie. They need time to talk."

Bernie's face drooped with disappointment. The hurt from betrayal shone in his eyes; even Morgan could not bear to see it. "Don't they understand Duncan risked his life for the people of this compound? Hell, he didn't even know who we were—"

At the bar, Bernie took a table and waved for the server, and Morgan sat with him. They were silent for several seconds. Morgan said, "I told you, Bernie, it's happening too fast. They're businessmen not fighters." The server stood next to the table. "Whiskey," said Bernie.

"Do you really think that's a good idea?" asked Morgan. "We're leaving early in the morning."

Bernie scowled at his friend. "I suppose you're

right." He looked at the server. "Change that to coffee."

"Make it two," added Morgan.

On the porch of their yellow clapboard covered house shined bright behind its white picket fence and ornate trim, which gave it a storybook appearance. Lisa, Bernie's wife, stood under her husband's arm with her head pressed to his chest; her blonde hair concealed her worried expression. They watch the sunrise.

Hitched to the railing beyond the fence were two horses; his saddle mount at nearly eighteen hands, and a pack horse laden with supplies and weapons.

Lisa looked up at Bernie; her blue eyes welled, but she didn't cry. "Promise me, you'll be careful." He tightened his grip around her shoulder. She persisted. "I want to hear you say the words, Bernie."

A great sigh issued from his lips. He said, "Lisa, you know I won't do anything that might keep me from comin' back to you—I promise."

Morgan reined in near Bernie's animals. He, too, led a similarly outfitted pack horse as did also, the four men with him. "Good morning, Lisa. You're looking pretty as always," said Morgan.

"Thank you, Morgan," said Lisa, a smile creased

her face. "It's nice to know that chivalry is alive and well." She elbowed Bernie, who smiled.

"Lisa, you know I think you're beautiful," said Bernie. "I guess, I should say it more, huh?"

She drew him down and kissed his cheek, which caused him to blush, but he didn't pull away. When Bernie stood, he looked passed Morgan; he saw Chuck Page, his mop of blonde hair bleached white by the sun. Reined in beside Chuck sat Mike Pizzolato. His black hair and olive complexion attested to his Italian heritage. Tom, (Tank), Shaw came next; he wasn't as tall as Bernie, but he was nearly as strong. The last of the four was Little Carl Johnson. Little Carl's father was Carl Johnson senior, a superintendent at the salt mine. The joke was that Little Carl was nearly the same size as Bernie.

Bernie glanced back to Morgan giving him a nod of approval for the men he'd selected. They each acquitted themselves bravely during the compound's attack by raiders, and also stood tall when they confronted Blackburn. "Well, I guess it's just going to be the six of us," said Bernie.

"Seven," called the approaching rider! They turned; it was Dan Fox a member of the council and the man responsible for the compound's security. "If you'll have me—I may be a bit, too, old for this business and don't want to hold you up."

A grin spread across Bernie's face. "I knew it, Morg. I just knew at least one of the council members would show up."

"We've got a long ride, Gentlemen," said Morgan. "I suggest we get started."

Bernie scooped up Lisa and held her gently in his arms. "We'll be back before you know it. Keep your fingers crossed—maybe we'll be attendin' Duncan's wedding."

She held his face between her hands and pecked his lips. "You just focus on getting back here in one piece that's what my fingers will be crossed for—now put me down."

He released her and moved down to his horse and mounted. "Why'd you clip the hair off your Clydesdale's hoofs?" asked Morgan a grin creased his face exposing his teeth.

Bernie looked down at his horse. "Huh?" he asked, staring now at Morgan, his brow furrowed with confusion.

Dan Fox sided Bernie. "He's got a point, Bernie. I feel like I'm riding a pony next to your horse."

Tank piped in, "Biggest danged horse I ever

saw. Where'd you get him—no foolin'?

Bernie sat erect with his chin jutted out with pride. "I've had Freeman at the livery lookin' for a while. Finally, a trader came through, and Freeman got him for me."

"Too bad he's a gelding," said Tank.

"Sorry, I said anything," said Morgan, and he led off and Bernie trailed looking back at Lisa. This was the first time since their marriage, they'd been separated; he already missed her.

Beyond the gates, they settled into a column of sorts. Morgan, Fox and Bernie rode three abreast. The rest of the men fell into a column of twos.

Two hours passed. "I think we should go faster," said Bernie. "It'll take forever at this pace."

Morgan's smiled reflected his tolerance for Bernie's impatience's. "It's a five-day ride to Coalville, and we want our animals in good shape when we arrive. Farmer and his men are at least three days behind us, so even if we rushed to get there we'd still have to sit and wait."

"I'll have to stop now and again to rest my butt," declared Fox as he squirmed on his saddle.

"That gets my vote, Dan," Agreed Morgan. "It's been awhile for me too, and my backside's not as tough as it used to be."

Bernie stood in his stirrups and flexed his butt trying to find a comfortable position, too, but didn't say anything. They stopped mid-day for coffee and food. Fox and Morgan exchanged looks when they notice Bernie hobbling about rubbing his lower back and butt. "Still think we should pick up the pace, Bernie?" asked Morgan.

"Ah, Morg, lay off will ya. I don't think I'll last five-days. That horse is big enough for my weight, but he has a stiff-legged gait and he's killing my back."

Fox laughed and the other chuckled, but they too rubbed their backsides for relief.

***

Two days later, a similar message from Duncan addressed to Farmer arrived at the Wyoming State Prison, where he, Theodor Bennett, was their council leader and driving force for change. Farmer met Duncan a year earlier when he rode for Ed Hayes, the leader of a gang of marauders. Ed unsuccessfully attacked Green River's compound, because he thought, they killed his brother Hank, and he wanted revenge. In the end, Farmer killed Ed in a gunfight and took over the prison. With Duncan's council, he turned the prison into the region's largest manufacturing center.

Married, he and his wife, Anita, now had two daughters, Diana and Morgana. Though challenging at times and certainly hard work, the rewards over the last year more than offset the trouble. He was reluctant to leave; though things were going well there was still an element of the compound that hungered for the old ways. His prolonged absence would give them an open opportunity.

"Theo," said Anita, "you should give the people of the compound, and certainly the council, your trust to take care of things while you're away. There is no possible way those holdouts from Ed's gang can take over."

Farmer gave her a weary smile. He already knew he was going, but—. "I worry about you, and the baby."

"We'll be fine and you know it, too. If Duncan needs your help, then go. We both know that if it wasn't for him, there wouldn't be an 'us' to worry about." She crossed her arms, and with an expectant stare waited for his response.

"I can't disappoint you and Duncan. I'll ready my gear and leave in the morning." He paused and looked once more at his wife. "I'll take maybe a half dozen men, but your brothers will stay here to protect you and help watch out for things."

"You know they'd rather go with you, Theo. Besides, it would make me worry less about your safety."

He sighed, and shook his head. "Alright, you win. I'll take Juan; he's the best fighter of the bunch, OK?"

Chapter 8

Five-days from Green River, Morgan and the others slowly rode into Coalville. They followed North Main Street south from Highway Eighty. It ran alongside a reservoir drained decades earlier leaving only the small flowing spring that once filled it. Forty-years of freezing and thawing disintegrated the paved roads; now a twenty-foot wide green belt of vegetation.

Tourism was Coalville's primary industry, which quickly disappeared when the Decline began. Empty timber-framed houses sagged to the ground. Many of the masonry buildings still stood; at least, their walls remained. Towards the center of town, the Mormon Temple's steeple speared up above the hollow shells of the other structures and was the only building recognizable. Instinctively, Morgan led them there.

"Duncan, riders are coming," called Rifle

Fielding, who stood lookout at Main Street's north approach. A quarter mile south, Juel Young, watched the road that allowed access from the Eighty.

As Morgan and the men reined in, Duncan came out of the church to greet them. They were city men not use to prolonged rough travel on horseback. There slow awkward dismounts brought humor to Duncan's eyes. Morgan stepped forward and offered his hand. "Morgan, it's really good to see you, thanks for coming." Bernie crowned to the front. "Bernie, my friend, I'm an uncle yet?" His friend grabbed Duncan into a bear hug and swung him around; Duncan cried, "Enough! You'll bust my ribs."

Dan Fox came next, but was more dignified with his greeting. He extended his hand and said, "It's good to see you again, Son. We're sorry to hear about your trouble—we're here to help. What do you need us to do?"

Duncan scanned the group though he recognized them he didn't remember their names. He made eye contact with each and nodded. Then he turned back to Dan Fox. "I haven't figured that out yet. I've been waiting for your and Farmer's arrival."

Morgan approached Fox and Duncan, he smiled and asked, "Where's the coffee?"

Duncan scanned the faces of his three friends. "Come on inside, I'll show you around and we can talk." Matt Wade stood by waiting. "Matt, would you please see to the new men."

Sitting at a table with a fresh brewed pot of coffee in front of them, Bernie asked, "Tell us what you've been doin' and where'd you meet Mary, what's she like, how old is she, and—"

Fox held up his hand for Bernie to stop. "Give him a chance to answer, Bernie. We got a day or so before Farmer arrives."

They drank coffee and talked for several hours catching up. Finally, they arrived at the main topic. "Tell us about Kimball," said Morgan, his tone professional and cold. Wade, who sat nearby, moved to join their table.

Duncan sat erect; he inhaled deeply, and began to speak, "Kimball is an insane and dangerous zealot, who believes he's a prophet of God. He's fixated on Mary, and her three sisters.

I met the girls just west of here; they'd escaped from their compound. The two youngest are twins who were only twelve at the time. Kimball claims to have received a prophecy from God that he shall marry all four girls."

"The leadership of their compound would allow such a thing," asked Dan Fox? "I mean laws have certainly relaxed and all, but not that far—"

"There is no leadership except Kimball," answered Duncan, his grave tone carried a sense of foreboding. "Anyone who disagrees with him disappears. Plus some of his followers evidently think he's really is a prophet and speaks to God."

"Why that's absurd," said Fox. "Surely, they don't—"

"They do," rebutted Duncan. "We have to assume the whole Henefer compound is dangerous and we shouldn't expect we'll find help there."

Fox scowled. "I disagree, Duncan. If conditions are as you suggest Kimball and his men won't find much support from the people. If we can draw Kimball out, or assassinate him—it'll be finished, and I doubt the people would lift a hand against us."

"So what's your plan then," asked Morgan?

The animated conversation attracted the others. One by one, they came and stood behind Morgan and Bernie to stare at Duncan; to learn how they were going to rescue Mary from Kimball.

Duncan sipped his coffee as he glanced over their faces. Addressing Morgan, he said, "When

Farmer arrives, I thought the three of us would ride up and scout their compound. We'd finalize the details after and then bring up the rest of the men. They'll have had time to rest and get things prepared."

Bernie spoke up, "What about me?" His tone and expression declared his obvious disappointment."

Duncan smiled at his old friend. "I want you to stay here and help Matt Wade integrate the men. Ours and Farmer's men aren't as—let's say organized." Duncan saw Wade standing back from the group and waved him forward. "Gentlemen, this is Captain Matt Wade, he's in charge of the volunteer militia group we brought from New Lovelock. Do you have anything you wish to add, Matt?"

"Only that we're very pleased that men of your caliber are joining the mission. This Kimball bunch is damned tough."

"He speaks from first-hand experience," said Duncan. "Whatever you do, don't underestimate Kimball or his men."

Over the days that followed, they soon developed a routine. They kept outposts far enough away providing an early warning to the main group, should they spot approaching riders. Their camp remained sparse; they could conceal their presences from anyone passing by within minutes.

As if on schedule, midmorning of the third-day after Morgan's group arrived, Farmer and five other men arrived. Everyone joined in to welcome them; they helped unload and stable their pack horses and provided hot coffee and food for the men.

Morgan stood and grinned as Farmer walked into the church. They shook hands; Duncan hung back for a few-minutes and watched while they acknowledged their unique history of being raised in a converted prison.

After the prison compound's raid on Green River, Farmer became their new leader. He changed the prison compound's attitude of surviving on what they stole to become a manufacturing center which prospered beyond anyone's expectation.

Finally, Duncan stepped forward; he noticed Farmer didn't seem as hard and lean as when they last met, but his handshake showed his grip remained firm. "It's good to see you again, Theo, or do you still prefer Farmer?"

Farmer smiled. "Even though I lead the council, most still don't know my name's Theodor Bennett— so just call me Farmer."

Duncan nodded. "Thank you for coming on short-notice—" He paused and swallowed to regain his composure. "And on such a personal matter; it means a great deal to me."

Still grasping Duncan's hand, he said, "It's I who should be thanking you. You changed my life. I have a family now and our compound is thriving beyond our wildest dreams. Now with the telegraph—"

"Telegraph!" Duncan glanced at Morgan. "You did it, huh?"

Morgan nodded. "We've only just begun. There's a line up to the prison and some of the other communities. We've printed a catalog of their products, and the surrounding communities place orders using the telegraph—"

The fact that Morgan used the word communities instead of compound wasn't missed by Duncan. "You should route a wire westward to New Lovelock. They are a huge agricultural community with a rail line to the west coast."

"Maybe we will when this business is settled," said Morgan. His words reminded everyone why they were there.

Farmer sobered. "Tell me what's going on."

Within minutes, they brought Farmer up to

speed. His questions were few and to the point. "I'd like to leave this afternoon," said Duncan. "We can camp near Henefer and scout their compound tonight and the surrounding area tomorrow."

Farmer excused himself to meet with his men and to get some sleep before they left. Morgan and Duncan gather the needed weapons and supplies and packed Duncan's mollies, Alice and Sophie. "These two mules are really something, Duncan," said Morgan. "Why you baby them more than most people do their pets."

Duncan grinned. "It's pays off in the long-run. They understand that I'll take care of them, and I know they'll go that extra mile for me."

"Just like your friends?" Morgan's comment and subsequent smile summed up Duncan's values.

"Yes, I believe friends are important. How would you survive without them?" Duncan saw Morgan glance over to where Dan Fox and Bernie were talking to some of the New Lovelock men.

"How indeed, Duncan—how indeed," asked Morgan; the formerly friendless man-in-black, who at one time expected to kill Duncan. Though it was less than a year past, it seemed long, long ago. He watched Duncan work and smiled at his friend.

They gathered at the cook fire around 3:00. They had a hot meal of canned meat with potatoes and carrots, a peach cobbler, and fresh brewed coffee; they expected it to be their last full meal until their return.

When they left Coalville, they headed out of town on the Main Street road. Henefer laid ten miles north on old Highway 84.

Duncan glanced at his Rolex, a gift from his grandfather before leaving Denver. "I expect we'll be in the area by 6:00. We'll set up a cold camp and wait for dark."

Clear of Coalville, a familiar sight appeared ahead of them. It was Lucky sitting in the middle of the road. Morgan's and Famer's horse bulked and refused to approach. Duncan and Buck with the mollies rode up to where Lucky waited. He dismounted and grabbed Lucky's hairy neck with both hands and they frolicked for several minutes.

Finally, Duncan stood. "Get off your mounts and slowly led them to us. They'll do fine once they've gotten a closer smell and see that he's not going to attack."

It required a full thirty minutes of indoctrination. The wolf sat patiently as the skittish animals came closer. Farmer's mare took longer to accept the wolf than did Morgan's gelding. After a while, she settled and allowed Lucky to walk behind her without being spooked and kicking. Lucky stayed with them for the next two-hours, and then slipped away.

"Where has he gone, Duncan?" asked Farmer.

Duncan watched Lucky disappear into the tree line. "He's taken a mate. I've named her Shadow; she has a white face with large dark shadows below her eyes." He smiled. "Evidently, they make her very enticing to Lucky. He's been with her for two-weeks now—I feared I'd seen the last of him."

Farmer laughed and poked at Duncan. "It was their honeymoon, Duncan. Just wait until we get Mary back, then you'll understand that new love has no time for anyone, or anything else."

Morgan watched the exchange and smiled. He'd seen it often when he rode with his brother Ed. The good natured ribbing took the edge off their pending danger.

Highway 84, constructed of thick concrete still remained. Freezing and thawing took its toll here and there, but the old road was easy travel. They rode abreast keeping to the northbound lanes, which put the median between them and Henefer. Once filled with manicured grass and wildflowers; nature has long since reclaimed the median. The thick stand of trees dense with underbrush provides good concealment for men wishing to avoid others.

A hand painted sign with an arrow pointing west announced they had arrived at State Road 65 and Henefer. Concealed under the road's overpass they made camp.

They'd just begun to unload their gear, when they heard the approach of several horses from the west. Each rider moved to his animals and held their heads and covered their muzzles to keep them quiet. The thunder of many horses at the gallop vibrated the overpass and rained sand and debris down on Duncan and his companions. Their passing noise concealed the muffled whinnies of the horses.

Farmer and Morgan exchanged glances as Duncan stared at the bottom the bridge. They're in a hurry," said Duncan to on one in particular. No one offered a reply.

It was still daylight and plenty of dry wood for a small smokeless fire. They brewed hot coffee; they would need it for the long night ahead. Farmer stood and absently swirled the last of his coffee in the cup, he finished it in a single gulp. "Think I'll take a ride."

Duncan looked up at Farmer, his brow pinch with curiosity. "It won't be dark for another two hours. You'll be seen."

Morgan let out a grunt. "That's his goal. Don't worry Farmer's an old hand at doing this. He'll ride up to their front gate; tell 'em he's traveling north and looking for shelter."

Farmer picked up the narrative. "One of two things will happen. They'll let me in for the night, or they'll send me on my way. If I get in, I'll scope out their operation. If they don't, I'll scout the compound's exterior." He laughed. "They'll ignore me 'cause I ain't sneaking about. Either way, I'll get more information than knocking around after dark."

"What if there's trouble," asked Duncan?

"There won't be, but if there is, I'm quick. A couple of rounds fired at the gate and spurs to the pony. I'll be back quick enough—no need to worry."

Duncan's scowl said he still wasn't convinced. "Listen to me, Farmer. The men inside that compound are harden fighters. They're coldblooded and will not hesitate to shoot—understand?"

"I appreciate the concern, Duncan, but I've done this before. If you'll remember, I'm reasonably good at talkin' my way out of trouble, or had you forgot?"

Duncan smiled at the gibe. "This is different, Farmer—"

"Let it go, Duncan," said Morgan. "Farmer is very good at this. His adversaries don't have a clue as to how dangerous he can be until it's too late." Morgan's grin was genuine, near laughter. "I've seen him charm the pants off of plenty of women and make their husbands glad he did."

"Yeah—what about the ones that didn't," asked Duncan?

Still smiling, Morgan said, "Like he said, he's quick."

The banter and subsequent laughter lighted the mood and Duncan's expression softened, and his shoulders lowered.

Farmer moved to the animals. He tightened the chinch of his saddle and then moved to his pack animal. "Just need to pack enough to look like a serious traveler."

Duncan pitched in, and together they had a well packed horse. As Farmer rode out of the camp, Lucky appeared from nowhere. He trotted over and lay by Duncan's bed roll and stared at Morgan.

Morgan stared back. Over his shoulder, he said to Duncan, "I think he still holds a grudge."

Duncan looked at them and began to chuckle. "I think it's you who has the problem. You still don't fully trust him and he senses it—he's suspicious." Morgan turned his back to Lucky, but he kept his head slightly turned towards the wolf.

***

Farmer's horse plotted westward toward the Henefer compound. As he expected; their gates remained closed, and two guards stood watch above. They scowled down at him as he approached. Both men dressed in identical black clothes; a uniform.

"Howdy," called Farmer, his toothy grin shined in the dimming light. "Lookin' for shelter—maybe do a little tradin'."

The man on Farmer's left spoke, "We're not interested—be on your way. It's too late in the day to dig a grave."

"Oh," said Farmer, his grin fading. "Listen, I don't mean to sound like I'm disputin' your wishes, but I've been on the trail for days and ain't seen a solitary soul. The conversation between me and myself has begun to get argue-some."

A low a chuckle, more of a rumbling noise, drifted down from the other guard. "What have ya got to trade?" asked the second guard.

"Well I tell ya, Friend, I got some salt and need supplies. You got a store inside?"

"Where from," asked the friendlier of the two.

"East of here near Denver; stopped at Green River to trade and ain't seen no one since. Don't you folks travel much?"

"What's the news?" asked the curious guard.

Farmer was going to gain entry. He may not be allowed to stay long, but he was sure he'd be invited in. "Well, Friend, that's part of givin' hospitality. You get to hear a bit of gossip and find out what's goin' on in the world—such as a traveler knows."

Mr. Friendly, as Farmer began to think of him, walked over to the other guard. It became clear they didn't have a clear-cut rule about travelers. Mr. Friendly won out. "We don't have a general store, but we do have goods for trade. After you're done trading, you'll have to move along—best we can do."

Farmer smiled. "Why a cup of coffee, or maybe somethin' stronger, and then I'll be primed for the trail."

The unfriendly guard scowled again. "This is a Mormon compound and you'll get nothin' stronger 'an water."

"My mistake, Friends," said Farmer. "I meant no

disrespect. Water will do me just fine—thank you kindly."

Mr. Friendly called down to someone inside and the gate began to swing open. Farmer heeled his mount and they rode through.

***

Long after dark, Farmer called, "Hello the camp—it's me."

"Come ahead, Farmer," said Morgan. "Duncan's wolf told us you were near twenty-minutes ago. What did you find out?"

"Plenty—" Farmer looked at Morgan. "It's a fortress; we don't have enough men or weapons to fight our way inside."

"Was there any sign of Mary," asked Duncan? The question drawing Farmer's attention from Morgan, he pressed, "Did you see where Kimball lives?"

Farmer turned to face Duncan. "There's an enclave inside the compound, with five-houses the one in the middle is the largest. It's my guess that's what you're looking for. It is west of their Temple, which is located along the east fence. You can see its steeple as you approach the compound."

A deep scowl formed on Duncan's brow as he

considered Farmer's information. At length, he spoke, "Mary and her sisters escaped from Kimball last year. They made it east fifty-miles to Evanston, Wyoming, where they met me. If they could escape the compound and evade Kimball and his men then, then I can get in and get them out. If we have a force waiting when I free them; we'll fight them on the plane. That'll even things up."

"There's one more thing you should know, Duncan."

"What," he asked?

"The only reason they let me into the compound is because Kimball and his guard are not there."

A quick smile came to Duncan's face. "That good news, they'll more likely to be lax. I'll just sneak in and get her before they realize what's happened."

Chapter 9

The snare Mary set before going to sleep yielded a fat juicy rabbit. Her stores depleted; she didn't have anything to enhance the meal, but it didn't matter. In her mind, this rabbit was heaven sent. Thankfully, Josh had instructed her how to survive in the wild, so after cleaning and roasting the rabbit over an open fire; she planned to stuff herself.

Tonight, it would be her fourth night since her escape. When she reached Riverdale, Utah, she intended to turn south and travel along Interstate Fifteen headed for the Eighty-Highway west. Beyond that, she had no plan. To get passed the salt flats and return to New Lovelock would require a horse and supplies. She would need help.

Hungrier than she thought; she'd eaten nearly all the rabbit. She lingered next to the fire. The three nights of travel under constant worry that Kimball would catch her had taken a toll; she was exhausted. Consuming the rabbit filled her belly and added to her desire to stay put and rest. Then night came, and its cold drove away the day's warmth. She couldn't risk a night time fire. Its light and smell would act as a beacon to her location. In the end, she decided to continue traveling at night. With a sigh, she gathered her few supplies into her bag, killed the fire, and started her night's journey.

Hours later, she guessed it was four o'clock in the morning; the cold settled on her shoulders like a heavy blanket. The tiredness clung to her legs making them leaden and harder to move. Near exhaustion, she leaned forward dragging one foot in front of the other to keep from falling. In the gray of the morning, she finally stumbled and fell; she could go no further.

She moved into the wooded median between the roads. As her habit dictated, she found the strength to set her snares. The sun peeked across the pine tops. The morning mist changed to vapor and drifted upward to the sky. In amidst the trees in the tall grass, much as a deer would do, she matted down the grass to insulate her from the earth below. Mary would feel the warmth of the sun's rays during the morning hours of her sleep.

The left-over rabbit was finished in four bites. Too tired to really be hungry, she curled up in her nest using her bag for a pillow. As the wave of sleep washed over her, she smelled the familiar odors of people. Riverdale must be close; she thought.

It was dusk when she woke with a start. Her senses returning, she realized; she must have slept for more than twelve hours. When she moved to rise, an involuntary moan slipped from her lips. All of her muscles and joints ached from the exertion. She desperately needed a day of rest, but could she risk a fire at night? Maybe she wouldn't need one; Duncan told her how to build a debris shelter. As she looked around, she thought, there certainly is enough material for one.

Fully awake, she stood. Walking about loosened her tired and sore muscles; soon she moved freely. The snares yielded a prairie hen. It had broken its own neck trying to escape the snare. Mary soon had a fire going and the bird hung on a spit roasting.

While the bird cooked, Mary gathered sticks and grass and whatever else lay about to use for her shelter. It wasn't much to look at; the sticks formed a framework on which she piled harvested grass, brush, and tree branches with leaves. One of the latter, she used for a door.

As with the rabbit the prior evening, Mary consumed most of the roasted bird. Sated, she crawled into her shelter; wigged in feet first was closer to the truth. She tugged the branch door into place and with her bag for a pillow, she drifted off.

Birds chirping and sounds of movement woke her. She rubbed the caked sleep from her eyes and peered through the tree branch door of her shelter. Several deer with fawns fed in the nearby grass. She remained in her shelter, now a blind, feeling warm and cozy, and watched nature's animals.

Finally, nature called to her, and she pushed away the branch covering her shelter's entrance and crawled out. The deer watched transfixed as she appeared from the ground. Then suddenly, as if per a well-rehearsed plan, they bolted across the little meadow and disappeared into the trees.

Rested, but stiff, Mary moved about to loosen her muscles. The exercise rid her of the morning chill she felt from being outside the shelter; she moved into the trees. Near the center of the median, she found a likely tree, an ancient pine taller than the rest with limbs offering an easy climb. She settled in astride a bough with numerous small branches which she twisted into a stable platform. From there, she ate the remainder of the fowl and watched the Riverdale Compound.

Mary didn't have a plan; she simply watched and hoped to see an opportunity that she could exploit. On road from the south, she saw them as tiny black dots, but something caused her to feel uneasy. Her eyes never left the dots as they grew to be riders dressed in black. Then, she saw the one-armed man leading the others; it was Kimball. In a panic, she looked around. Could they see her hiding in the tree, would they think to look up?

She watched them get closer and like the deer of that morning, she wanted to bolt from her hide and vanish into the trees below. Reason took hold, and she calmed her fears. If she remained perfectly still hugging the tree's trunk, she wouldn't attract their attention.

As they closed on her perch, she closed her eyes and held her breath; much like a child who thinks if she can't see them, they can't see her. The burning in her lungs caused reality to return, and she opened her eyes. When she looked, she saw Kimball staring at her; her heart leaped to her throat, and she froze with fear. Then just as suddenly, his stare turned away.

She felt weak; glad that she'd built the platform for she surly would have fallen. The adrenaline rush subsided, and energy slowly returned to her limbs. Mary watched as Kimball and his men rode toward the Riverdale Compound. Kimball's visit with the elders of Riverdale would prevent any chance of her receiving help there.

When her strength returned she climbed down from the tree. Her feet planted firmly on solid ground, the tension released from her body. She stretched followed by a yawn; the fear she experienced from seeing Kimball left her exhausted.

Regardless, she had to have a plan of action if she was to evade Kimball and his men. She burrowed through the wild flora of what was once a golf course to a spot where she could see the road without being seen. Whichever way Kimball took, she would go the other way.

***

Kimball, followed by his guard, rode through the gates of the Riverdale Compound. It resembled many of the other small compounds built around Salt Lake City. Its forted walls constructed of timbers culled from the nearby forest. Their temple, cloistered by mid-twentieth century houses, became the heart of their community.

Elder William Ivey stood outside their temple's administration wing to greet him. Ivey's lanky 6'-9" stature was deceptive. He weighted near three hundred pounds and was as strong as two men. His wavy silver hair was at odds with his youthful face. The clinch of his square jaw and the direct stare from his pale blue eyes foretold of the mettle within.

"Elder Kimball," said Ivey, "it has been many years since we've had the pleasure of a visit. What brings you here?"

Kimball watched as Ivey's glance lingered at the stump of his right arm, and he caught the slight flicker of the elder's eyes when he saw Kimball's mutilated face. A crooked smile spread across Kimball's face. The scars, which froze the right side of his face, made his features even more grotesque looking. His dark eyes flashed when he spoke, "My bride-to-be, Mary Evans, has been kidnapped."

Ivey's shrewd eyes took in every detail of the men mounted before him. Kimball's missing limb and scarred face conveyed signs of recent trouble; the details of which did not yet reach his compound. "I see," said Ivey. "No one has stopped here recently—certainly no women." He paused for Kimball's response. Hearing none, he continued, "Won't you dismount, rest your animals, and join us for a meal?"

Kimball looked around as if just now noticing where he was. His eyes blinked several times as he struggled to make meaning of Ivey's words. Finally, James, one of his guards moved forward and spoke quietly. "Leader, do you wish to stay for a meal with Elder Ivey? He's right; the horses need a rest."

His eyes focused on the compound's elder, Kimball said, "Thank you, Elder Ivey, I will. It's been a long ride, and we are tired." Absently, Kimball cupped and vigorously massaged the stump of his right arm. Ivey stared; Kimball saw and smiled half apologetically. "The palm of my right hand itches."

"You'll of course be a guest in my home. We'll find accommodation for men with—"

Kimball interrupted Ivey. "That will not be necessary. They will be outside the compound searching for Mary. I expected you to provide addition men to help. If she came this way, your compound is the only place she could find help."

Ivey's brow pinched, and his eyes squinted as he studied Kimball. "I thought, you said she'd been kidnapped?" There was hesitation in his words as he continued, "We've heard things, unpleasant things about your compound, Elder Kimball."

The scar on Kimball's face flushed pink, as he stared at Ivey with hooded eyes. "You—"

James quickly stepped to Kimball's side and whispered in his ear, "Leader, this is not the time or place."

The distraction was enough; Kimball blinked several times, softened his expression and relaxed his shoulders. With the fingers of his left hand, he combed his long stringy hair away from his face and forced a cockeyed smile. "The nonbelievers carry lies about us all, Elder. I certainly don't believe the ones told about Riverdale." Ivey's stare showed he remained unconvinced. "Mary is a clever girl. If she is able to escape, she will. They know we're after them and they may be close by. If we had help from your people, she might call out—"

Ivey continued to stare at Kimball for several heartbeats, and then with a nod; he turned. "My home is this way." He glanced over his shoulder to confirm Kimball followed.

Robert and Eliot, his second guard, escorted him to Ivey's home. At the door, Kimball paused glanced at his guards. "Elder, will you give us men to help search?"

Ivey looked passed them to four men who'd discreetly followed. "Benjamin, you four go with Elder Kimball's men and do what you can to be of service."

Kimball nodded to James, who turned and headed for the main gate and their horses.

***

As darkness stole the daylight, all Mary could see was the dim aureole rise from the Riverdale Compound. She felt the cold settle across her shoulders and wished for the warmth the glow promised. She hadn't eaten since early morning, and her energy had depleted; hunger pangs nagged her stomach. Not since Duncan found her, and her sisters, had she felt so starved.

Until she saw Kimball earlier, she had planned to be on the road, but now …. She needed to know which way he traveled before she decided her next direction. If he back tracked toward Henefer, then she would go south on Highway 15. If he went north, she would still go south. Should Kimball choose to go south on Highway 15, then she'd give them a day or so head start and follow. So for tonight all she could do is wait and watch.

When the glow over the compound diminished, she made her way back to the debris shelter. Soon, her heat loss slowed and she began to feel warm; she fell asleep.

A noise; the sound of men talking awoke her from a deep sleep. Light streamed through pin holes in her shelter's walls. Her heart raced, and adrenaline surged through her veins as she fought panic and tried to think. What did her shelter look like, she couldn't remember? When she built it camouflage hadn't been her motive; she just needed a place to stay warm. She focused on the steps she took to build it. It was a simple A-frame low to the ground with leafs and bunches of long grass loose layered to form an insulated burrow. It would blend into the background from a distance, but if someone walked up close to it ….

Mary could make out the words of two men talking. "What are we supposed to do with this girl if we find her? You've heard the stories about Kimball same as me. She wasn't kidnapped—she escaped if you ask me."

The other voice said, "You heard Elder Ivey. We're to be of service and help them search. He didn't say anything about returning an escaped bride to Kimball."

They stopped talking and Mary heard them walking around her shelter; she held her breath and waited.

"Ahem," said the second voice. "Miss, if you're in there and need help because you've been kidnapped and want help make a noise."

She lay perfectly still, but she still sensed their presents. "Please go away, I don't want to be forced to marry Kimball." She spoke so softly, she wasn't sure she'd actually said a word.

The first voice said, "We understand. I'm leaving my canteen and some dried fruit. Stay in there at least another hour, we'll be gone by then."

Her fear arrested, and tears of relief began to flow down her cheeks, she said, "Thank you."

Mary waited longer than an hour; she waited until the sun was up and beating down on her shelter. It became uncomfortably warm. Finally, she eased the branch door away from the opening and peered out. To her left sat the canteen, and paper folded into a package. Pulling the package to her, she exposed its contents; dried apple slices and apricot halves.

She took a bite of dried apricot, and its natural sugar caused her to salivate. The canteen came next it was nearly full plus now she would have a container to carry water. She ate several more pieces of fruit. As the glucose entered her blood, she felt its energy invigorate her wellbeing. Her ability to think clearly returned. On her elbows, she crawled free of the shelter. She inched up near the edge of the tall grass and surveyed the meadow; they were gone; she remained undetected.

Low to the ground, Mary crept back to the trees. Once among the trees, she felt safe enough to stand. There was no one near, so she climbed the tree of the day before and settled down on the platform she'd built. From there, she began a systematic survey of her surrounds and the Riverdale Compound.

The gates were open and people moved in and out freely; unlike the Henefer Compound. She wondered if Kimball remained, or had he departed? If he left, which direction did he travel? Mary allowed her fear of capture to hold her inside the shelter longer than necessary. She chastised herself and swore not to let it happen again; her survival and freedom may depend on it.

Watching the sun's rise to the east, she guessed it was mid-morning. Mary decided to wait until noon before choosing her next move. She didn't have long to wait. Within half an hour, Kimball and his guard exited the compound's gates. They rode with purpose; their direction of travel decided: south on Highway 15. She would stay put one more day and then follow their course.

Snares needed to be set if she was to eat. She thought it strange, her feeling of wellbeing. Then it occurred to her that knowing Kimball's direction of travel and approximately his location made her feel safer than she'd felt in days.

The area's wild game was plentiful and evidently not over hunted. Her second snare produced a plump rabbit, which she roasted over a small smokeless fire built among the trees. To her the aroma of wafting away as the rabbit cooked seemed so strong, she feared it might cause someone to investigate.

Mary spent the remainder of the day in her tree-top nest watching the comings and goings of the Riverdale compound. How different her life would have been if only her compound had been like theirs. Then, she thought of Duncan and her regrets vanished in an instant.

Evening came and Mary returned to her shelter. As she lay letting her body heat warm the space, she reflected on the words of the men who'd left her the canteen and fruit. Could she trust the people of Riverdale? Would they help her?

Chapter 10

The crescent moon's subdued light worked both ways; Duncan could make out the terrain and see where he was going, but they, if they were on watch, could see him, too. Morgan and Farmer hid in the tree line on guard to cover his escape, or retreat. Lucky lay in the tall grass next to him.

Duncan decided behind the temple would be the best location to breach the wall. "Is the way clear, Lucky" asked Duncan? He stroked the wolf's mane.

Lucky lifted his head; his nose sniffed the air, and his keen sight stared at the compound's wall. He rose and loped across the open area. Duncan followed, his only burden a knotted rope. At the base of the wall, he uncoiled the rope and tied a huge knot into one end. Prepared, he stepped back into the open area and whirled the knotted end several turns; its speed and force increasing with each rotation.

Finally, he released his grip on the rope, and the knot sailed over the wall. With care, he pulled the rope's slack to him until the knot lodged into one of the many gaps between the wall's post.

After several tugs bouncing his full weight on the rope, he was satisfied it would hold. He jumped up and grabbed a knot and began the slow hand-over-hand climb to the top of the wall. Lucky made a low whimpering sound and began pacing where the rope's end lay on the ground.

"Lie still; Lucky, I'll be back soon enough" The wolf did as bid and lay near the rope's end. He crossed his paws, and lowered his great hairy head to wait. A snorted huff noted his displeasure and caused the nearby grass to wave.

Perched on top of the wall, Duncan retrieved the rope and tossed it to the ground. Lowering himself, he silently dropped beside the rope. As he coiled the rope, he surveyed his surroundings and listened for movement. Hearing nothing, he moved to the boxes stacked against the temple's wall. He tested their weight, they were empty. He relocated several making a stairway of sorts for his and Mary's escape.

The compound was asleep except for the guards at the gate and men patrolling the houses. Curious, he thought: are they protecting the occupants or guarding them?

After several minutes of observation, it became clear the guards were accustomed their routine; they were lax. He kept to the shadows, and made his way to the fence outside the Leader's house. Accessing Kimball's enclave was easy. A great oak with overhanging limbs grew inside the fence. With a quick toss of his rope, he captured a limb and was up and over.

Poised higher in the tress, Duncan studied the back of Kimball's house. Compared to the other homes it was a mansion. The entire structure was constructed of white limestone, with a slate roof. It was old, built before the Decline.

Duncan continued to study the house, and then, a creak. He froze and focused on the direction where the sound emanated. A window slid open and a woman's voice spoke, "Who's out there—Mary?"

The use of Mary's name startled Duncan. It was dark in the shadow of the tree, and he couldn't make out who, or how many people there were. He considered for several seconds and finally, he said, "I'm a friend of Mary's."

A woman leaned through the window into the

moonlight. Duncan could see that she was an older version of Mary. The same pale skin, blonde hair and though he couldn't see them, he knew she had light blue eyes, too; were they related?

Her voice lowered to a husky whisper; she asked, "What do you want?" Duncan heard a tinge of fear in her voice; was he in danger?

He was committed and wouldn't turn back now. "I'm here for Mary," said Duncan. "Where is she?"

Judith glanced about and seeing no one else, she said, "Come in."

There was no hesitation. If it were a trap, so be it. Inside the bedroom, he asked again, "Please, where is Mary Evans?"

Judith stared at him for a long time; Duncan tried, but could not fathom her thoughts. Finally, she spoke, "Mary escaped two nights ago. The scouts he sent out returned this morning. Leader left earlier this evening to bring her back."

Duncan wasn't sure if he was glad or concerned. To be away from the insane John Kimball, he was thankful, but it meant she was on her own trying to survive without the necessary means.

"Do they know which way she went?"

Judith's gave him a wry smile. "They found

where she went over the wall behind the temple, but that's all they found. Leader took enough men to go north and south."

"Do you have anything that Mary's worn and hasn't been laundered," asked Duncan as he looked around the room.

Judith's confused expression softened with the understanding of why he wanted her clothing. "Yes her sleeping gown. It's in the other room; I'll get it."

Duncan's hand snaked out and grabber her arm, his firm grip and icy stare conveyed a message. "You needn't worry;" said Judith. "I'm the one who helped her escape. I'll be right back."

When she returned, opened her bedroom door, and stepped into the room, the young man was nowhere to be seen. She stood motionless and confused; a hand touched her back, and she started dropping Mary's gown bringing her hands up to cover her mouth. Duncan swung the door closed and stepped out of the shadows. "Just being careful; sorry of I scared you." He looked down. "Is that the gown?" Still unable to speak, Judith nodded. He picked it up and looked round the room. "I need something to wrap it in that won't contaminate Mary's scent."

"I have butcher's paper I use to wrap my clothes in for storage. There's a roll in the closet."

With a nod, Duncan walked into the closet. The sound of paper tearing said what he was doing. He returned with a sheet about two-feet square. On it, he laid Mary's folded gown and wrapped it tightly in the paper, which he tucked inside his shirt. Ready to leave, he said, "Thank you—what's your name?"

"Judith." She gave him a faint smile.

Ready to leave, he stopped at the window, and turned back into the room. "Why do you stay? Why does anyone stay with this compound?"

She offered another weak smile and shrugged. "It wasn't like this in the beginning, but now we're afraid for our children."

He nodded his understanding and stepped out onto the tree and disappeared into the darkness below. Her eyes blinked several times and then an expression of confusion spread across her face. What an unusual young man, she thought, why would he care about us? Especially, after the Leader kidnapped Mary; he should hate us.

Duncan dropped down the wall outside the compound. Lucky waited, and his tail wagged his greeting. After a mandatory tousling the wolf's coat for a greeting, Duncan stood and trotted to the tree line; Morgan and Farmer waited.

"Where's Mary," asked Morgan?

Farmer added, "What happened?"

"Good news and bad." They looked on expectantly. "Mary's escaped," they smiled, "but Kimball is after her. It was him we heard riding overhead earlier."

"Which way did they go," asked Farmer?

"They don't know, so they've sent two groups. Kimball's leading one, but I don't know which."

"Which way do we go," asked Farmer?"

A huge grin spread across Duncan's face. The first they'd seen since arriving; he pulled out the white butcher paper and unfolded it revealing its contents. Farmer smiled nodding and glanced at Lucky, and said, "A four-legged road map."

"Wait here, I'll be back in a few minutes." Duncan led Lucky back to the compound fence and let him take up Mary's scent from the gown. The scent is strong. Duncan thought: I think he remembers her, least I hope so.

Within minutes, Lucky had her trail and loped off eastwards toward the tree line where Farmer and Morgan waited. Just before entering the trees, he turned north and broke into a run. Duncan followed, but detoured at the tree line for his friends and Buck. "He's got her scent."

As they mounted, Farmer gave Morgan a smile and a nod. "It'd be perfect if we got her back without a fight," said Farmer. "To tell the truth, I've gotten soft. My back's stiff and I can't feel the cheeks of my ass—for all I know they've worn off."

An amused expression softened Morgan's face. Listening to Farmer's complaints finally made him chuckle, he said, "I'd forgotten how much you liked to carryon about your misfortunes."

"You tryin' to tell me you're the same hard-man you was a year back," countered Farmer.

Mirth remained in Morgan's voice. "To the contrary, but I'm a happier man, and for the first time during my life, I've begun to think about old age; maybe I should get married and start a family."

It was Farmer's turn to be amused. "Now there's a picture for ya—don't you think, Duncan. A bunch of little Morgans running loose; why I bet they'd have the entire compound terrorized."

A scowl caused Morgan's face to droop, but his eyes still twinkle with humor. "At least they'd be boys—not like the harem you've begun to rear. How many girls are there now? Is it six?"

Enjoying the banter, Farmer clutched his chest. "Morgan, you wound me. I've got two girls, which you very well know. Why we named the second girl Morgana after you—you're such an ingrate."

Morgan's face sober and he stared intensely at Farmer. "You never told me about that—why?"

Farmer looked ahead at Duncan's back. "Well, if you rode up for a visit now and again, you've of known. As to why—"

Duncan, who listened to their conversation smiled. Morgan, based on a past friendship spared Farmer's life when Farmer, as a member of the marauders attaching the Green River Compound, gave himself up and told Morgan the details of the gang's plan. Farmer feeling grateful named his next child after Morgan.

"Up ahead," called Duncan, interrupting their conversation. "Lucky's lost her trail at the stream."

They watched as Lucky began making larger and larger circles around the point where Mary entered the water. Farmer sided Duncan's right and Morgan came up on his left.

"It appears she's learned a bit about breaking her trail. I'm impressed." Farmer lifted his brow as he smiled at Duncan.

"Yeah," said Duncan, "She paid attention when we escaped from Kimball the first-time." A sense of pride sounded in his voice.

Out of sight for several minutes, Lucky appeared on the other side of the stream. He turned to leave, then stopped and look to make sure Duncan followed. They crossed the water and trotted their mounts in pursuit of Lucky.

The wolf followed the stream for over two hundred yards, and then abruptly; he turned north angling back to the tree line in the highway's median. They traveled for eight hours. When they came to where Mary made camp it was daylight.

"She's moving at night and sleeping during the day," said Farmer after he spent several minutes inspecting her campsite. "She must have a small kit and food supplies—see here where she prepared food. She's not defenseless—"

Duncan grinned at Farmer. "She can use a throw stick and she knows how to set snares, too."

Morgan and Farmer smiled indulgently at Duncan. "You've instructed her well, Duncan," said Morgan. "Can she fight too—if it comes to that?"

The smile left Duncan's face and his shoulders

slumped. He looked northward as if trying to catch a glimpse of her. "Not like you mean, Morgan. Besides, I doubt if she arm with anything beyond a kitchen knife." His brow pinched in thought. "We rest the horses for couple of hours and then start out again." Morgan and Farmer nodded. Farmer tended to the animals while Duncan started a fire and brewed coffee.

Chapter 11

Lucky's nose was infallible. Even when Mary crossed streams, or traveled on hard surfaces where the morning fog condensed and diluted the scent, he found it again and again. It was Duncan, Morgan, and Farmer who had trouble keeping up with him during the night.

"Duncan, it's too dark to follow," said Farmer. "We're lucky not to have gotten knocked out of the saddle by a tree limb, or injured one of the horses. Let's make camp and start again at first light."

Duncan rubbed his face with both hands trying to clear his thinking. He knew Farmer was right, but ….

"He right, Duncan," agreed Morgan. "We can do her little good if we're hurt, or afoot."

His shoulder's sagged as he sighed. He inhaled deeply and said, "I know you're both right, but if we miss her—"

Farmer took the lead and guided them toward the sound of running water. On the south bank of a stream, they found a clearing and made camp. They wanted coffee, so they decided a fire was safe enough. Kimball was north of them, and if Mary were close by, she might come to them.

They were efficient, and had the horses hobbled and coffee boiling within twenty-minutes. Farmer poured Duncan the first cup. Duncan leaned back against his saddle and sipped the dark strong brew. He hadn't eaten for hours, so the caffeine sped through his veins, and his thoughts began to clear.

His companions were right to stop until daylight. Hopefully, they'd make better time and make up for the hours lost resting. His cup was empty, so he filled it again. Farmer had unpacked some elk jerky, and they had something to fill their bellies besides hot coffee.

"What do you think, Farmer," asked Duncan?

Farmer stared at Duncan's face for several seconds before he answered. He was good at reading people and situation. "I think we'll know something by late-afternoon tomorrow."

***

With the morning came Mary's resolve to enter

the Riverdale compound to ask for help. But there was reluctance as well; she stalled. She spent her morning checking her snares, which provided a fat juicy rabbit. No longer concerned about a fire, she soon had the animal cooking on a spit. Assuming she'd soon be inside Riverdale's compound, she ate the entire meal.

She lay back to enjoy the full feeling in her stomach. The warmth radiating from the fire made her sleepy; her lids felt heavy and she nodded off and didn't hear the footsteps.

"Are you Mary Evans?" asked the man. His voice startled Mary awake. "Take it easy young lady. It's me, the man who left the canteen and food. I just come out to see that you're alright."

Mary gripped the hilt of her knife, such as it was, with the intent of lashing out if he reached for her. Looking up and seeing his face and hearing the softness of his voice, she pulled back her hand. "You gave me quite a scare, Mister."

His warm smile and quiet voice lowered Mary's guard. She accepted his offered hand as she attempted to stand. As he helped her to her feet; without warning, he struck the point of her chin with his fist. The blow dazed her senses, and she began to collapse. The man caught her, hefted her across his shoulder, and carried her to a pair of waiting horses.

When Mary recovered her senses, she found herself wrapped in a tarp and tied to a saddle across the back of a horse. She moaned, and then asked, "What's happening?" The man didn't answer. She struggled to escape the tarp and get her bearings. Judging she'd only been unconscious for a short while, she deduced their direction of travel was south. Her question was: is it Highway 84, or the 15?

She couldn't see the man, or his horse, but she could hear them. Finally, the man spoke, "So, you're awake." He halted his horse, and dismounted walked back to her. Lifting the edge of the tarp, he said, "I'll release you and sit you up in the saddle if you promise to give me no trouble."

"Where are you taking me?" she asked. Though, she already guessed the answer, she had to hear him speak it.

The man's smile remained pleasant. His attitude was as if he were escorting her to a social function. Using his best manners, he said, "I figure Kimball will pay handsomely for your return."

Stunned, Mary said nothing; she could only stare

at the man. Untying the ropes, he handily unslung her from the horse and allowed to walk around to loosen the stiffness of her muscles. As she moved about, she considered her situation.

Though she'd never seen Highway 15, she was pretty sure they were on southbound lanes of Highway 84. She wondered how the man expected to catch up to Kimball. She asked, "The Leader and his guards are on highway 15—you're on 84?"

His pleasant demeanor continued, he said, "Kimball returns the long way taking Highway 15. Even at our slow pace, we'll be there several days before he arrives." The bewildered expression on Mary's face made the man chuckle. He said, "I've no wish to deal with Kimball out in the open. He'd kill me without a moment's hesitation."

"What makes you think it'll be any different at the Henefer compound?"

Again, he chuckled. "I've got family who lives there. He won't want to needlessly cause trouble amongst his followers."

This time it was Mary, who chuckled, though it held no humor. "Were I, you, I wouldn't count on that. The Leader is ruthless; he'll kill you if he wants and no one, family or not, will stop him." She watched him closely to measure his reaction. He turned and stared. He tried to gauge her words; she smiled. "On the other hand, if you help me return to my family in New Lovelock; they'll reward you and allow you to stay and start over fresh."

The man didn't respond. She gave him time to ponder his situation. Finally, he asked, "How long would the trip take?"

Mary stared westward for several minutes before answering. When she spoke her voice was warm, friendly, and her expression relaxed. "Three weeks, or more, I think. Of course, I'm sure my people are out looking for me, so it could be less time."

"Three weeks!" It was the first time she'd seen him show any real animation. "We don't have enough the supplies, and then there's Kimball to deal with. He's between us and your New Lovelock."

"What's your name anyway, asked Mary?" She'd begun to think of him as Mr. Average. He was average in everything: Age, his dull brown hair and eyes, his pasty white skin, his height and build, and his demeanor. There was absolutely nothing notable about this man. Though, time spent with him was under circumstances that she was sure, she'd always remember; she'd be hard-pressed to describe him to anyone other than average.

"Joseph Smith," he said.

"Really, you're kidding—right? Why not use John?" asked Mary with skepticism thick in her tone.

His answer was the first time she noticed any show of heated emotion. "Because, my parents named me Joseph," he said, his voice agitated his face colored with anger. Mary had pushed a button. His name really was Joseph Smith and based on his reaction; he must have been teased badly about it.

"Oh," she said her tone now apologetic. "Were you teased a lot as a child?" She watched him closely as he responded.

He took several deep cleansing breaths, and his sudden anger passed. "I was an only child. My mother doted on me and well—"

"The other kids were jealous—right?"

They rode side-by-side, though he still held the lead to her horse. Her hands were tied to the saddle horn, but she wasn't uncomfortable, so acting friendly towards Joseph was easy. When he looked at her, searching her face for guile, Mary smiled.

Seeing Mary's friendly face, Joseph's guard began to lower. "That's what my mother always said—they were jealous of me because our name was Smith, and my mother named me after our Founder."

Joseph, with Mary's encouragement, began telling her the story of his childhood. He told of the slights of the other children, his mother's untimely death he was fourteen, and his father's apparent disinterest in him. This was especially true after his father remarried and started another family.

Hour after hour as they traveled, Mary began converting Joseph into an ally.

***

At first light, Duncan stoked the fire and brewed coffee. Farmer and Morgan crawled stiffly from their bedding. There were audible cracking sounds as Farmer stretched to loosen up. "Damn, Farmer, just how soft have you gotten?" asked Morgan, who was occupied with rubbing his own back.

"It's age more 'n anything else—" Farmer chuckled, and then added, "You know I continued leading a rough life long after you left to find an easy job as a lawman."

Morgan's eye glanced at Duncan. "I wasn't always a lawman, Farmer, but I'll give it to you that I led an easier life after I left the prison, and I damn sure don't have any regrets."

Farmer also glanced at Duncan, who seemed not to be listening to their conversation. "Nor, I, Morgan, things have been good—"

"Coffee's ready. You want any?" asked Duncan offering the pot. These biscuits will be ready soon." He nodded at Farmer, and asked, "How about fryin' some bacon?"

They set to finishing breakfast, breaking camp, and readying the horses for travel. Lucky circled the camp confirming Mary's scent and nudged Duncan's leg to hurry.

By mid-morning, Lucky circled a large meadow. Beyond the meadow's northern tree line, lay Riverdale; the first place Mary might have gone to seek help since her escape, but Lucky didn't leave the immediate area. They dismounted and watched him work.

Eventually, Lucky found her shelter. He stopped searching and lay by its doorway and whined. Farmer, the better tracker between he and Duncan, knelt to inspect the ground. "She spent a couple of days at least here. Look at the fire ring and the animal bones."

By the different soot markings, Duncan saw that she'd built small fires to cook the game she'd snared;

two rabbits and a wild bird. "She stopped to eat and rest. Her supplies from Kimball's compound must be gone. He poked through the animal bones with a stick; she'd picked them clean.

Duncan watched Lucky, how could the wolf lose her scent—where did she go? She just didn't fly away, or …. "Kimball must have her!" said Duncan.

Farmer and Morgan stared at him for several seconds, and then Farmer began to circle her shelter in an ever widening circumference. "Here, Duncan." Farmer pointed to the ground. "Horse prints; a man dismounted and walked to the shelter. When he returned his prints are deeper, he's carrying Mary."

"Which way did they head?" asked Morgan. He scanned the horizon as if he hoped to see something, or someone.

Farmer knelt to inspect the horse prints. "Two horses rode in from the west and return the same way."

"They can't have been gone all that long—look how sharp the prints are. The grass is still bent and the animals haven't disposed of those animal bones. Let's mount up!" said Duncan.

"Maybe longer than you think Duncan," said Farmer. "Let's check at Riverdale and see what we can discover."

Twenty minutes later, riding at a gallop, they arrived at the Riverdale gate. Though the gate was open, they would not be allowed entry without answering questions and stating their business.

Though Duncan was the youngest of the trio, but moved forward as their leader. "This concerns a young woman, who has escaped from the Henefer compound. Her name is Mary Evans. We're trying to find her before John Kimball does." The curious expression that grew on the guard's face caused Duncan to ask, "What do you know? Is she inside? Has she been here—tell me?"

Duncan's voice grew louder as he spoke. Morgan sided Duncan and put a restraining hand on his shoulder. "Duncan, let the guard answer."

The guard had already begun to step backward and strengthened the grip on his rifle against Duncan's perceived aggression, he said, "The girl hasn't been here. Brother Kimball came looking for her and left yesterday morning headed south."

"Which road?" asked Duncan.

The guard looked to his right. "Why, he took Highway 15. He believes the girl went that way—he searched the eighty-four."

Duncan led off south toward the Highway 15, he said, "Let's get back to where Lucky lost her scent and see if he can follow the horses," said Duncan. "That's our best chance."

***

Mary came awake, but didn't open her eyes. She lay completely still and listened. She heard only the normal noises of nature at dawn. Birds chirped as they moved through the bushes searching for food. Squirrels leapt from one tree to the next making the canopy alive with movement. When she opened her eyes, turned her head and stared across the campfire, she saw Joseph curled into a fetal position beneath his blanket. The study movement of the bedding told her he remained asleep.

After last night's behavior, she still wondered what she should do. So long as she was free and out of his range to grab her, she felt confident that she could escape if needed. Her equestrian skills were better than his …. Finally, she decided to see what the day would bring. If he still seemed dangerous, she'd escape with one of the horses and take her chances alone.

She rose quietly and slipped off into the woods for her morning duty. On her return, she was very noisy, which startled Joseph awake. "What?" he asked. As he flailed about trying to get free of his blanket. Mary watched as he finally emerged the winner. Still disorientated, his back to her, he said, "Don't try to escape you know you can get away."

"Really, you should have told me an hour ago. It's time for you to get up if you want to eat. The horses need attention."

Joseph turned to see Mary standing by the fire with a fresh armload of wood. He stared at her for several seconds, his face blank of any indication of what he might be thinking. Finally, he said, "Why didn't you try to escape?"

Not wanting a recurrence of last night, she answered quickly and without any sign of concern. "You promise to take me to New Lovelock. I can't get there without help, so why would I run?"

Her response must have been the correct one. He shrugged and walked off toward the horses to move them to water. When he returned from his chores, Mary had breakfast cooking and fresh coffee brewed, which she poured when he sat.

"We're late in starting our day," said Mary. "Do you still think we can pass by Henefer without a problem?"

Joseph blew on the hot coffee before sipping. After a few sips, he responded, "Even if they're watching the road, all they'll see is a couple on horseback riding south."

Mary gave his comment several minutes of thought. "I guess that's true." She chuckled at the situation. "They would never suspect it was me riding by in broad daylight."

"Our greater concern is Kimball returning to Henefer." Joseph stared southwards. "If he stops at every compound along highway 15, it'll be several days before he swings east and back here."

"But what if he goes west instead hoping to catch me before I get to New Lovelock?" asked Mary.

Joseph's head snapped up; his face ashen as he stared. "I hadn't thought about that—he'd be between us and New Lovelock." The fear that grew in his eye conveyed what he was about to say. "There's no way around him—he'll catch us—" Without finishing his coffee; he rose and began to pace.

Mary watched him and saw a change in his eyes. Hoping to soothe his growing edginess, she said. "He'll run into the militia from New Lovelock—they're bound to be searching for me."

"But what if they're not?" He stopped pacing and

looked at Mary, and he saw the fear growing in her eyes. "Don't worry, Dearest, I won't let him catch us. Well go north and swing down highway 15; he won't go back that way again. Maybe we'll like one of the compounds—we can start a new life together."

***

Lucky circled the area several times; returning to Duncan after each attempt. Duncan sent him back out to search again each time. Finally, Morgan said, "He's lost her scent, Duncan. Let's move south until we catch him. If Kimball's found Mary, we'll get her back. Even if he hasn't got her, we'll deal with him and resume our search for her."

"That makes the most sense," added Farmer.

Duncan sighed as he stared first at Farmer and then at Morgan. His eyes shone with the disappointment he felt. He looked down at Mary's shelter and said, "We were so close." His arms hung at his sides, and his fists were white knuckled. "I shouldn't have stopped looking for Kimball the first time until I found his body, or killed him." When he looked up at his friends, they saw a rage growing in his eyes neither would ever suspect him capable of.

"We'll camp here and get a fresh start at sunup," said Morgan. He looked at Farmer, who nodded.

Duncan said nothing, but he didn't resist as they led him to a clearing to make camp.

Duncan operated on auto-pilot, he unsaddled Buck and helped with the pack animals and even gathered wood for the fire, but only after he'd sat awhile and sipped a cup of fresh brewed coffee did he speak. "When we catch up to them, I'll deal with Kimball. I just need you two to help me get a clear shot" He sat down his coffee and stepped over to their gear and retrieved his Winchester 30-06 pump rifle. From its case he removed the tools and solvents for cleaning. The light was poor, but he'd done it so many times, he could have done it in the dark.

Farmer watched him for several minutes. Finally, he asked, "Do you mean to kill him from ambush?"

Morgan watched Duncan for a heated reaction to Farmer's question, but none came. Instead, he remained calm. Morgan could feel the cold fury as he continued to clean his rifle.

Duncan looked up at Farmer. "If I can get a clean shot—yes, but I still plan to put a bullet in his head up close and personal."

Farmer and Morgan exchanged glances. This was a cold inhuman side of Duncan; they would have never believed possible. Morgan said, "Duncan, that's a hard thing to do and even harder to live with. Once it's done, you can't go back."

Farmer nodded his agreement. "It's one thing to kill during a fight, but another to kill him in cold-blood without a chance."

A humorless smile creased Duncan's face as he looked at Morgan. "I understand, but this isn't the first time. Morgan when your brother kidnapped Lisa, now Bernie's wife, we tracked them and waited until they bedded down. Then we kill them in their sleep. There was no remorse—they needed to be executed."

Morgan's brow pinched as he looked at Farmer for confirmation. Farmer nodded. "I found the camp, Morgan. It was a bloody scene—they didn't have a chance. Though—" He paused and looked at Duncan. "I guess you didn't have no choice since you were outnumbered. That was hard, Duncan, you must have pure steel for balls."

"Hank was one of my two half-brothers by a man who raped and abused my mother after he kidnapped her. He was only slightly less a bastard than Ed. I agree with you; they needed killing."

As if he were compelled to say something, Farmer added, "There weren't no love lost between me and Ed either, but he had more of chance than

Hank and his boys when I killed him."

A weary smile came to Morgan's face. "OK, so were all three hard-men who can kill without remorse. I guess it's the times—"

Morgan and Farmer sat quietly watching Duncan clean the Winchester. There was something comforting in the way his hands moved. Each motion seamless followed the next without wasted motion. When he was done, Duncan chambered a round, ejected the magazine and replaced the shell.

The process must have had something of a therapeutic aspect to it, because when Duncan replaced the rifle in the case, he seemed less cold— more his old self. He exhaled, and his shoulders lowered. After long a stretch, he poured another coffee. "I think I'll turn in when this is done. Sunup comes early—."

Until now, Lucky stayed clear of their camp, but when Duncan relaxed the wolf came into the fire light and lay at Duncan's feet. Farmer shivered. "How long did it take you to get use to him sneaking around that way, Morgan?"

"Who told you I was used to it?" They all laughed and when Lucky looked from one to the other with a tilted head, they roared with laughter.

Duncan grabbed two hands full of Lucky's neck fur and gave him a hearty rubbing. "They're just jealous because you're better lookin' than them."

As Duncan predicted, sunrise came early. Farmer stoked the dying ember of their campfire and soon had a blaze pushing back the morning's mist. All three sat on their haunches arms resting on their knees warming their hands. "I'll make coffee, but I made breakfast yesterday," said Farmer.

"I'll cook," said Duncan. "Morgan's not thin by chance."

"Yeah," added Farmer, "if I had to eat his cookin' I'd be downright skinny." He and Duncan chuckled at the scowl Morgan gave them.

Morgan stood and turned his back to the fire. "Poor cooking skills have kept me away from the chore for a good many years." He walked away from the fire to attend to nature's needs.

As he watched Morgan walked away, Duncan said, "He's laughing at us."

"I knew it all along," said Farmer. He and Duncan chuckled.

When Morgan returned, Duncan had biscuits baking in their Dutch oven, and Farmer was frying bacon and beans. "I'll start breaking camp—seems only fair since you made breakfast." Farmer and Duncan wordlessly glanced at each other and smiled.

By the time the sun was up full, they were ready to ride. Duncan was in the lead with Morgan beside him and Farmer behind them leading the girls, Sophie and Alice. Lucky led off and within minutes disappeared over the horizon.

Farmer watched as Lucky loped away. "I bet he can run like that all day, and there ain't no way someone's goin' to set an ambush for us with him about." He turned to Morgan. "Could've of used him in the day—uh, Morgan?"

Morgan sobered. "Those days don't hold any fond memories for me. If you thought it through, Farmer, I suspect they wouldn't for you either."

"I only meant—" Farmer shrugged.

Duncan didn't listen to their exchange. His thoughts were focused on catching Kimball; had the zealot recaptured Mary? "Kimball's got a two-day lead, but I figure he'll stop at each compound to make inquiries if he doesn't already have Mary. If we stay in the saddle all day, we should make contact with him by nightfall."

Chapter 12

"We must've of missed her, Leader," said James. "She couldn't have made it this far alone and on foot. Besides none of the travelers, we've spoken to report seeing anyone fitting her description."

Kimball stared at his guard for several long seconds, his head slowly nodding. "I agree, James." He looked southward down the 15 and then to his guards. "We've checked the Roy compound, so we'll split up from here. James, you and I will ride to Bountiful you other five will each go to separate compounds and see if she has stopped there for assistance. Whatever you discover, ride to Bountiful and report." The men waited attentively as the Leader assigned their compounds. As he pointed, Kimball named them: Sunset, Clearfield, Layton, Kaysville, and you take Farmington."

"You heard him—move out," commanded

James; they turned and as if spurred the horses bolted southward at a gallop.

Three hours later, Kimball and James waited outside Bountiful. Had his guards found Mary? As soon as the question entered his mind, it left. If they'd found Mary, they'd have sent word. He needed to be patience. Mary had taken the 15, he was sure of it; his anticipation began to grow.

One-by-one, his guards returned; each empty handed. Kimball's disappointment transformed and then began to culminate into a rage. His guards, all except James, kept their distance not wishing to bear his wrath if the last man showed up without the girl; the guard from Farmington still remained absent.

***

Highway 15 was no different than any other road across the country. It decomposed, and there are long sections where nature has reclaimed the byway as ribbons of grassland. It's on grass-covered earth that Farmer can read the signs of Kimball and his guards. The progress is slow, but constant.

Dismounting, Farmer stooped to inspect the hoof prints. "They stopped here—see how the prints form a circle?" He stood and walked a few paces southward. "They've decided to split up." Farmer lifted his hat scratched his scape; his confusion clearly shown in the expression on his face.

Duncan, who'd studied the road map, had a better understanding of what lay ahead. "There are several small towns between here and 80. My guess is he's sending a man to each." A smile creased his face. "—which means, he doesn't have Mary."

Lucky, who'd been circling the trio searching for Mary's scent and guarding their back trail appeared. Farmer watched him keenly as the wolf inspected each set of prints. Finally, Lucky trotted off following the two sets that rode together.

Farmer let out a chuckle as he shook his head. "Don't know why you wanted me to come," he nodded after Lucky, "your wolf doing fine without my input, maybe better."

"Well, he can't talk, so why don't you tell us what he's up to," said Morgan. He didn't smile, but humor shone in his eyes.

Their spirts were lifted with the knowledge that Kimball still hadn't caught Mary, so the banter continued. "You're right, he can't talk—I'm redeemed." Even Duncan laughed softly. "What the hairy beast is telling us is—that Kimball and one of his guards ride alone. My guess is they're goin' to meet up later somewhere down south."

"Mostly likely where the 15 and the 80 join. — how much of a head start do they have," asked Duncan.

Farmer examined the prints. "I'd say a half-day— there abouts.

"If we rode hard could we overtake them before they join his other men?" asked Duncan.

Stroking the neck of his horse and judging its condition, Farmer swung into the saddle, and said, "It's worth a try."

At the sound of galloping horses behind him, Lucky set off at a run leading the group. Duncan felt confident that the wolf's nose would alert them in advance of any possible ambush.

An hour or so later, Lucky's pace slowed, and the riders did likewise. When the wolf stopped, Duncan moved up and dismounted to stand near him, so he could speak softly. "Are we close?" asked Duncan. He scanned the road ahead. Seeing nothing, he returned to Buck, retrieved his binoculars, and climbed to an outcropping on a knoll that was once a highway median.

As he focused the glasses, he saw a single thin stream of smoke rising beyond a high grade in the road. It has to be them, he thought, why else would Lucky have stopped. He re-cased the binoculars and hurried down the knoll to his waiting friends.

"If you squint you can see a stream of smoke." Duncan pointed southward. Farmer and Morgan both stood in their stirrups.

"If you say so," said Morgan. Farmer added a shrug.

For the first time in his young life, Duncan felt excited about killing someone. It wasn't hatred for Kimball. Except for the trouble he caused Mary and her sisters; Duncan cared nothing for, or even gave the zealot any thought. One foot in the stirrup, his hands on the saddle ready to pull up, he hesitated and asked himself why?

Morgan and Farmer exchanged glances. Morgan asked, "You alright, Duncan?"

Duncan didn't answer, but the question interrupted his thinking long enough for him to mount Buck. He sat out at a slow walk and continued to probe his motives. If he removed Mary from the scenario, Kimball was just another man; granted he was a bad man, but not one Duncan wanted to eliminate from the face of the earth.

It was Mary's safety. He now understood the

emotion that Bernie felt when Lisa was kidnapped. Only Kimball's death would insure her complete wellbeing, and Duncan was ready to oblige.

Farmer reached out and touched Duncan's arm. "We're close enough—how do you want to handle this?"

Lost in thought, Duncan jumped with surprise. "I, I'm not sure." He wiped his face. The action seemed to clear his mind. "We need to find out how many men are there, and then plan our attack." He paused, and then added, "If I can get a clear shoot, I'll kill Kimball from ambush. I don't care about the others."

Morgan, who knew Duncan best asked, "Are you sure you can live with that—I mean cold blooded murder from ambush?"

When Duncan looked at Morgan, his expression held no stress, or worry. His face was smooth, and he appeared somewhat naive. "Kimball is a mad-animal; he's ruthless with his people; he's murdered, and he's after Mary. Yes, my conscience can live with killing that bastard from ambush—I'll sleep fine."

Nothing further was said. They dismounted lead their animals among the trees of the median and tied their leads to saplings. "You two stay here," said Farmer, "and I'll scout their camp." Within a few yards, Farmer disappeared into the forest.

Duncan moved to his pack mule, and fetched his pump-action Winchester 30-06 and mounted its scope. Morgan watched his methodical unhurried movements; they made him seem cold and unfeeling, which indeed he was. By the time Farmer returned, Duncan had field stripped the rifle, cleaned and inspected its operation and fed ammunition into its six magazines of four rounds each. "One in the pipe plus six magazines that tallies to twenty-five rounds—think it'll be enough," asked Morgan.

"If there's a firefight, you let me know after—"

Farmer drew near. "It's Kimball and five of his men."

Duncan nodded. "How's the camp lain out?"

"They're in a clearing just off the road on this side of the highway. Kimball, the one-armed guy dressed all in black, is closest to the fire, and his men move about as you'd expect." He looked up at Duncan. "I got a good look with my glass—he's one ugly son-of-bitch. Your wolf do that?"

"My pistol got his arm, and Lucky got his face. We thought he drowned, but—" Duncan straightened and slung his rifle over his shoulder. He looked at his Rolex, and said, "I make it 6:30. You two cross the road and work your way down across from their camp. I'll go down this side at 7:00; I'll kill him. If the others try to make a fight of it, then you two join in— they'll be in a crossfire. That should take the starch out of them."

Morgan and Farmer picked up their long guns and moved out. Duncan started south through the trees with Lucky on his heels; within twenty-minutes, Duncan was in place. He saw Kimball setting on a log holding his left hand out to the fire for warmth. His guards were done with their camp chores and they also sat around the fire.

Duncan checked his watch; five-minutes to go. He was behind a tree that provided cover and a forked branch to support his rifle. The shot was maybe seventy-five yards; he didn't need the scope, but he wasn't taking any chances. Three-minutes; he dialed in the scope and practiced sighting. He would put two center-mass and try for a head shot to be sure. One-minute; Kimball was speaking. Duncan couldn't make out the words. Kimball spread his stump and left arm wide and looked skyward. He must be praying; Duncan mumbled, "How appropriate." Lucky let out a low growl. Five-seconds; Duncan sighted, safety off, finger on the trigger, exhaled, and gently squeezed.

In that split second, several things happened. The rifle fired; James moved to stand in front of Kimball, and Lucky broke cover and rush towards their camp. Duncan chambered the next round. When he re-sighted, he saw James falling into Kimball pushing the zealot backwards behind the log.

***

The remaining guards dove behind the log where James lay atop Kimball. James was dead; Duncan's bullet severed his spine. The Leader struggled to remove James's body, but the other guards held him still. "Don't move, Leader—James's dead. We're under attack." Kimball froze, and then said, "Don't be ridicules—I command you to get James off me."

Eliot, James's second said, "Leader, please. Didn't you hear the rifle shot? We're being attacked."

Kimball stopped struggling to digest the information. "I don't hear any shooting."

"Someone's out there with a rifle and you're his target," said Eliot. "If James hadn't moved in front of you, you'd have caught that bullet. Now please stay down."

"As you will, but get James off me," commanded

Kimball.

Eliot and another guard grabbed James's jacket and tugged. Inch-by-inch, they dragged the dead man off the Leader. "That's better," said Leader. "Now I can breathe. What do you see out there—any movement?"

"None," said Eliot. "He's waiting for another shot." Eliot surveyed their situation and quickly made a plan. "We need to slip into the darkness and find cover." He pointed to two of his men. "Little Bob, you and William get the horses and swing around to the south. We'll mount up and head for the 80 and the rest of our men." Eliot and Richard crawled dragging Kimball with them into the darkness. Soon they were among the tree behind cover. Kimball stood first and brushed debris from his clothes.

Kimball looked into the darkness and saw two glowing yellow orbs fixed on his movements. He back to a tree and clawed at its bark with his one remaining hand. There was something familiar about their size and color, and then he remembered; they haunted his nightmares. Those eyes belong to the wolf that mauled his face.

"Kill it," screamed Kimball pointing at the darkness.

Eliot and Richard both turned just as Lucky sprang, and they fired their guns. The wolf was dead before he reached Kimball following inches short of his prey.

Kimball stared down at his demon frozen with fear. Finally, realization came to him that it was dead, and he began to savagely kick the dead wolf yelling, "Demon, demon—"

Eliot had to pull him away as Little Bob and William arrived leading their horses. They mounted and prepared to make a break when shots rang out from across the road.

"There's more than one," said Little Bob. "Stay low."

***

Morgan and Farmer heard Kimball's scream followed by two gun flashes, so they opened fire on the location. Without a sure target the best they could do was empty their weapons.

***

Unknown to them was Lester Johns, the last of Kimball's guards en route from Farmington. Hearing a gun shot, he halted to assess the situation. He could see the fire, but no one sat nearby. Then, he heard a scream and two more shots coming from the trees beyond the campfire. In the dim light, he saw two men step out from cover and began shooting into trees where the scream and shots emitted.

Pulling his 1911 Colt .45, he fired off three quick shots at the two men. A split second later, he spurred his mount and bounded for the campfire.

Eliot looked up as Lester galloped by the fire, and seeing who it was, he yelled, "Hold your fire; it's Lester." They finished mounting and chased after him leaving Duncan, Morgan, and Farmer to deal with the aftermath.

***

Duncan was the first to the tree where Lucky lay. He dropped to his knees and cradled the wolf's head in his lap. His eyes welled with tears that soon streamed down his cheeks. "It's my fault, Boy. I should have told you to stay with me, but I was so damn anxious to kill Kimball—"

Morgan ran up and seeing Lucky, he said, "Sorry, Duncan. You two were best friends, I, I—" He couldn't think of anything else to say that would be remotely comforting.

"Morg—" It was Farmer. He slumped forward on his knees near the waning campfire; his hand probing his left shoulder.

Morgan started for his friend. "Duncan, Farmer's been hit."

Gently, Duncan lowered Lucky to the ground and followed Morgan to see about Farmer. "How back is it," asked Duncan?"

"I took one in the back. It was a guard coming back from one of the compounds, I guess. The slug's still in there—it burns like hell," said Farmer. He appeared ashen and about to faint as he looked at Duncan. "Do you think you can get it out?"

Duncan rolled him over. "Morgan build up the fire, so I can see better." He pulled out his boot knife and cut away Farmer's clothing. Morgan did as instructed, then left and returned with their animals. "There's a first-aid kit in my saddlebags." Morgan rummaged through the bags and retrieved the kit.

With clean gauze and water, Duncan washed away the blood to inspect the wound. There was a high-up finger-sized hole behind his left shoulder blade. Farmer's breathing seemed stable and there was no blood, so it missed his lung; it continued to bleed.

"Well?" asked Farmer. "Can you get it out?"

Duncan shook his head. "I'd need to wait 'til morning for the light, but we don't have time. Kimball will regroup and come after us. I'll pack the bullet hole and put on a field bandage, and then we'll get you the next compound for medical attention."

While Duncan worked on Farmer, Morgan took a small shovel from the pack mule and began digging a shallow grave. He and Duncan completed about the same time. Duncan looked back at his friends dead body and sucked in several deep breathes to check his emotions.

Farmer said, "Duncan, a few minutes aren't going to a difference with me, or Kimball. You take your time and bury Lucky." Duncan hung his head for several seconds, and then rose and slowly walked to stand by Morgan.

Morgan had laid Lucky's body on a tarp. They pulled the body into the hole and folded the canvas over his body. While Duncan filled the grave, Morgan carried pieces of broken concrete from the highway and stacked them close. "We'll place these over the grave to keep out predators."

Duncan had no words; he reverently placed the first piece of rubble on the grave. Morgan followed his lead until the grave was covered, and Lucky's body protected.

Morgan left Duncan at the grave and went to

wait with Farmer. In a low voice, Farmer said, "I wouldn't have thought anyone would have gotten that attached to a pet."

A humorless chuckle; a noise that seemed more like a grunt sounded from Morgan. "He and Lucky were trail mates. That wolf saved his life more times than you can count. He wasn't a pet."

Several minutes passed without conversation as they watched and waited. Finally, Duncan rose from the grave site and joined them. He looked down at Farmer. "We need to get you to the closes compound and get your shoulder seen to."

They helped Farmer mount his horse and headed north.

It was slow going to Farmington. Their compound sat three-quarters of mile east of Highway 15 passed an abandoned amusement park whose skeletal remains reminded Duncan of prehistoric beast. Like most of the Mormon compounds, it was built around a temple. Six square blocks of houses were barricaded behind their temple.

It was just after midnight when they approached the gate. "Halt!" sounded the guard from a perch above the gate. "State your business and keep your hands where I can see them."

Morgan raised his hands. "We have an injured friend and need medical attention. Will you help us?"

The guard called to someone below and after several seconds a man-door in the gate opened and different guard exited and approached. He stared at Farmer slumped forward in his saddle. "What's happened to your friend?"

Not wanting to get into the details of their situation, Duncan offered, "We were ambushed a few miles south of here."

The explanation seemed sufficient, as the guard turned and called, "Best wake up the doctor." As the guard walked back to the gate, it swung open admitting Duncan and his troop. The guard led them to an ancillary building near the temple; it served as the compound's infirmary. They collectively gathered around Farmer and eased him from his horse and conveyed him inside.

***

Once they were sure there was no pursue, Kimball and his remaining guards slowed their mounts. Eliot said, "Leader, Richard thinks he shot one of them, so I don't think we're being followed. We should make camp and rest. We'll find the others tomorrow and then go back for James's body."

Kimball's eyes darkened as he stared at Eliot. "James's soul has begun it journey; I care not for his remains. We will rest tonight, and tomorrow you will find the others. Then we shall pursue this man Duncan and end his blasphemous life."

Chapter 13

"Matt," said Bernie. "Somethin's happened. Duncan should have reported back by now."

"I've been thinking the same thing, Mr. Olsson."

Bernie smiled at the young man. "I've asked you to call me Bernie. When you call me Mr. Olsson, I get confused about who you're talkin' to—OK?"

"Yes, Sir—I mean yes, Bernie."

Bernie slapped Matt on the shoulder nearly knocking him off his feet. "That's better. Now—about Duncan not reportin'."

Matt's jaw set as he came to attention, he said, "Duncan's orders were for us to remain here until he sent for us."

"I know," said Bernie, "but, he should have sent word by now." He turned to Dan Fox. "What do you think, Dan?"

Fox glanced at Matt. The determination chiseled

on the young man's face was easy to read, and then he looked back at Bernie. "I believe we should wait as Duncan asked, but maybe, we could send a scout as far as Henefer to confirm there's been no trouble."

Bernie stood. "I'll get saddled."

Matt's eyes darted to Fox. It was clear he wanted Fox's help with dealing with Bernie. Fox rose also. "Bernie, I was thinking we'd have Mr. Wade send one of his men to investigate."

"But, I want to go. If Duncan's in trouble—"

"If Duncan's in trouble," interjected Fox. "You'll bull your way into the situation and create an even bigger problem. Let one of Matt's men go—I'm sure if he's seen, he'll blend in and won't be noticed."

Bernie's shoulders fell, and his expression turned sullen. "Well maybe you're right about blendin' in, but I'd never do anything to cause danger for him."

Fox smiled at his big friend and put a hand on his shoulder. "I apologize, Bernie; I misspoke." He nodded to Matt, who turned and marched away towards his waiting men.

As Fox and Bernie looked on, Matt gave instructions to one of his men. The man saluted and went to the makeshift corral to ready his mount. Matt returned to where Fox and Bernie waited.

"I've sent Bagley; Lon's a good man," said Matt. "He's to return before nightfall—sooner if he finds any sign of trouble."

***

The scenery along the highway became monotonous; tall green pines with dark impenetrable undergrowth lined the road without change. In a way, it made Joseph's dialog interesting by comparison. Mary listened and consoled, so by the time Mary and Joseph stopped to make camp, Mary's hands were no longer tied. They were friends; at least, that's what Joseph thought.

Her hours of listening to Joseph's miserable life story, and her show of empathy won him over. She felt bad for misleading him about how much she really cared, but she would do just about anything to escape the clutches of John Kimball. Besides, if he actually helped her reach New Lovelock; she'd be grateful and would be his friend and assist him to start anew.

"We're close to Henefer," said Joseph. "If we start early tomorrow, we should be able to ride by without being noticed."

"So you'll help me return to New Lovelock?"

Joseph stared at his feet for several seconds. He

answered without looking up. "I'll do what I can, but if Kimball—"

"Sure! I wouldn't blame you, but don't think about that now. We'll get passed him and when I get home, I'll introduce you as my friend, and you can start a new life." Mary was being positive for her benefit as much as his.

They were camped in the median where a rest stop once existed. Nature reclaimed most of the area, but there were patches of concrete the forest hadn't yet taken back. Without being asked, Mary help Joseph unpack their supplies and set up camp. Joseph erected a canvas tent; a pup tent really, but it provided shelter against the night air.

Mary, meanwhile, slowly circled their site collecting dried wood for a fire. Before long, she had a fire going and started preparing their meal. "You're experienced at this kind of living aren't you? I mean that shelter and the game you caught—"

She thought of Duncan and her sister. "My fiancé, Josh Duncan, taught us how to live off the land." She glanced at Joseph and saw that his expression changed.

"Josh Duncan?" he asked his tone flat and without feeling.

Meanness appeared in his eyes; he gave her a cold penetrating look. It made her skin crawl; she'd gone too far with charming Joseph over to her side. He was jealous. She quickly remembered the things she'd said to him; there was nothing she said that would really give him the wrong idea. Surly, he wasn't so lonely that he would misinterpret civil kindness; it was only friendly conversation.

"Yes, he's the man who found us after we escaped from Kimball." She felt defensive. "He killed two of Kimball's guards to keep them from taking us back—they were very bad men."

His face softened and when he spoke there was a pleading quality to his voice. "But, I thought you liked me and when we got to New Lovelock, we'd—"

"Joseph, I never said anything to give you an idea like that." She closely watched his face; he was thinking. The cold eyes with no expression returned.

"I thought you were different from all the rest, but you're not. You're making fun of me just like the others. You think they'll laugh when you tell them, well they won't find out."

Mary's eyes grew wide as she dropped the spoon used to stir the beans, and she stepped back from the fire. He's crazy, she thought. She fought the impulse to run. If she did, he would catch her and then what—?

She steeled herself. "Joseph, that's not true and you know it! I'm sorry you've misunderstood, but I haven't intentionally misled you—I'm not like the others. I do want to be your friend." She watched him closely. The next move was his, she prayed he would get hold of himself and calm down.

His face slowly reverted to its calm expressionless features; a mask which concealed his true feelings. He sat on a nearby log and watched the fire. Mary retrieved the spoon from the pot and continued preparing their meal. Finally, he looked at Mary. "I suppose you're right. You haven't said anything that I could consider a direct statement, but you've hinted."

Only when she exhaled did she realize she'd been holding her breath. If she were honest maybe she did imply there was an interest. She'd do just about anything to avoid being returned to Kimball and the horrible life that would surely follow.

She gave him a smile, but her expression and pinched brow conveyed there was no humor, or romance. "If I did that, I'm sorry. It is not my intention to mislead you. I just want to be friends and when we get to New Lovelock, I'll be your friend and introduce you to other people who will want to help you too."

"Why?" He was angry again. "You're saying that just to get me to help you. When you get what you want, you won't want to be my friend then—will you?"

Now Mary's temper began to rise. "Joseph, I'm not that kind of person. Have I tried to escape, or done anything but help?" Not giving him time to respond, she continued, "No, I haven't."

Joseph smiled. "You're prettiest when you're angry. I'll have to learn how to tease you, so I can see how pretty you are."

That made no sense; what is he talking about? "What—"

"It's OK, Sweetheart. After we're married, I'll only tease you now and again." He held out his plate. "Is the food ready?"

Mary was too stunned to reply. Obviously, something had snapped in Joseph's mind. What should she do? Her instinct was to say nothing further; she neither wanted to encourage, or anger him more than he was at present. Maybe rest would help the situation. She filled his plate and poured him coffee.

She couldn't eat; as she chewed, the beans

formed an insipid paste that seemed to grow larger. Mary sat quietly in the shadows of their campfire. Hoping not to exacerbate the situation further, she didn't speak, or look at Joseph.

He did not seem to notice her present except to lay his plate, cup and spoon at her feet when he finished eating. She quickly gathered them, and along with her own; she scurried down to the water. As she worked, she stole a glance over her shoulder at Joseph. He'd prepared his bedroll and sat pulling off his shoes. She gathered the dishes and watched.

After a huge yawn, he lay back and appeared at once asleep. Mary's mind raced as she reviewed her options. She could steal away into the wood cross the road and disappear into the night. Her woodcraft skills were superior to his; besides in his present state, he might forget about her entirely. The horses nickered catching her attention; she could knock him in the head with a rock and take the horses. A pang of conscience pulled at her, and she dismissed that choice. Lastly, she could remain in the hopes that rest would correct his thinking, and that he would honor his promise to take her back to New Lovelock.

Likewise, too spent to think, she selected the easiest path. She would stay and see what the morning brought; she didn't feel he was dangerous to her physically.

***

It was dusk, and Bernie paced the floor; the stomps of his heavy footsteps echoed through the empty room. Nearby, Matt Wade watched, his own apprehension growing in his mind. "Lon should return soon," said Matt.

Bernie halted and turned on Matt. "It's near dark—where is he?"

"Rider coming," called a voice from outside.

Matt smiled at Bernie. "Right on time—"

Bernie scowled, but said nothing as he turned to the doorway.

Lon Bagley marched through the doorway. Upon seeing Wade, he snapped to attention and saluted. "Reporting, Sir—"

Wade returned the salute. "At-ease, Bagley—report."

Bagley stood easy and glanced at the fire and pot of coffee.

"Get a cup of coffee and sit down, Boy," said Bernie.

Bagley glanced at Wade, who nodded.

"Thank you, Sir," said Bagley, and he moved to

the fire to pour himself some coffee, he squatted holding the warm cup in both hands. After a sip, he began his report. "There's not much to tell. I sheltered my horse under the overpass and climbed a tall pine that gave me a good view inside the compound and the surrounding countryside." He drank more of the coffee; its heat dissipated into his hands. "Inside their compound things appeared normal—no one entered or left."

"What about Duncan and the other," asked Matt?

Bagley nodded as he finished the last swallow of his coffee. "There was sign of a fresh campsite below the overpass. Had to have been them—no reason for a traveler to camp there when the compound's a quarter of a mile away."

"Nothing more?" asked Bernie.

Bagley looked up at the big man and saw the concern in his eyes. He paused and concentrated, then added, "Well, north of the compound; I saw a couple set up camp in the median. It seemed strange they didn't continue to the compound—" He shrugged, and then glanced at Wade.

"Thank you, Bagley," said Wade. "That'll be all for now."

Matt watched Bagley poured another cup of

coffee and leave the room. He turned to Bernie, but the big man spoke first, "Where are they—what's happened?"

The young officer didn't speak for several minutes. Bernie returned to pacing. Finally, Matt said, "I can only see two possibilities. First, they were caught and are prisons, or dead; or second; Mary and/or Kimball are not there, and they've gone searching for them." Matt glanced at Bernie, who'd, stopped pacing to listen, and his face flashed with disbelieve. Interpreting Bernie's expression, Matt added, "I agree, Bernie—it's highly unlikely that anyone, or anything could kill all three of them and leave no evidence."

Bernie's massive shoulders lowered like an animal settling down to rest as he exhaled with relief. "You've got that right," said Bernie. The immense smile that followed spoke to the amount of worry and concerns the giant carried for his friends. The big man found a spot and sat. He let his mind relax, and memories came to him of what he and Duncan experienced when they rescued Lisa, his future wife. They never spoken of the slaughter that took place that night.

***

Duncan tracked Lisa's kidnappers and set the plan. If Bernie had been left on his, he and Lisa would have died that night. He was nervous until he saw Lisa's unconscious figure tied to a tree like an animal. A cold rage settled in and there was no stopping him then. The recalled memory still felt raw, as if it happened yesterday. It was like he watched from afar: Bernie's arm darted out from behind the tree; he clutched the guard by the throat, and snatched him back into the woods.

Bernie held him by the throat in his huge left hand. Feet off the ground, the guard clawed at Bernie's forearm and kicked in desperation at his capture. Bernie's wrath had been unleashed and with all his fury, he swung his fist down on top of the guard's head like a great hammer hitting an anvil.

Bernie's blow drove the guard's skull down onto his vertebra breaking his neck at the brain stem and killing him instantly. Like an angry bear, Bernie shook the guard and seeing the limp body flop like a rag doll, dropped it to the ground.

Duncan was only a heartbeat ahead of Bernie stepping out of the woods, weapons in hand. Without warning, they executed the sleeping men before they became fully awake. In quick succession, he shot the three men closest to his position, and Bernie shot the remaining two.

When the shooting stopped, there was a sudden and deafening silence, except for the high-pitched ringing in their ears. The smell of cordite mingled with the smoke from the campfire was acute, almost overpowering. They stood motionless for several heartbeats staring at their deed.

After, they rode in silence the entire trip back. Bernie cradled Lisa in his arms, and that is where she would stay until they reached their camp. Duncan dealt with his demons after he had killed those men. Bernie was absorbed with caring for Lisa.

***

Wade removed from his satchel a yellowed road map and unfolded it with care; its brown creases dotted with holes. He sat at the table and began to study the routes. "They've gone north up the 84. If they'd gone south, they'd have stopped to update us and give new orders." He paused and looked up at Bernie, who'd moved to stand across the table. "The basis of our original orders has changed—"

Bernie stood fully erect. "Well then—let's go find them."

Matt smiled patiently at Bernie. "Without the

knowledge of what motivated them to change the plan—we wouldn't have a chance of locating their direction of travel much less finding them."

"What do ya think we should do then," asked Bernie?

"I've been considering that problem."

"Well," said Bernie.

"Well," repeated Matt, "assuming Mary is gone, or not arrived and Kimball and his men are out looking for them, now would be a good opportunity to take over his compound." Matt watched Bernie as he absorbed his words.

"We can't just attack their compound—we don't have enough men," he began, "What about the innocents who live there?"

Matt raised his hands to stay Bernie's further comments. "Correct, we don't have an army, but if what Mr. Fox said about the compound is true—then the number of men we have is enough."

Bernie scowled. "You're not makin' sense."

"Think about it, Bernie. If the compound is ruled by Kimball and his guards, and he with a portion of guard is away searching for Mary, then his forces at the compound are weakened. With some help from us, the people might revolt and become our army."

Matt watched as Bernie considered the possibility. Finally, he asked, "So how do we get in and make contact?"

"I haven't worked that out yet, but let's get Lon in here and see what he has to offer regarding the compounds features."

Twenty-minutes later, Wade, Bernie, Dan Fox, and Lon Bagley sat around the map making plans on how to infiltrate the Henefer compound. "We need a ruse to get some men inside to talk to the people and a way to sneak in once we're ready."

Dan Fox looked through the doorway across the street to the building where they stored their supplies. "I think Matt and I could trick our way in pretending to be traders. We certainly have enough goods to play the part."

Bagley sketched the Henefer compound's layout and surrounding area. "Getting inside unseen shouldn't be a problem." He pointed to a location on his map. "Here behind their temple, we should be able to get six-men over the wall undetected. If the compound works with us, there might not even be a fight."

Matt, the tactician of the group, said, "OK, here's what we're going to do. Mr. Fox, you and I will leave first thing in the morning; Bernie, you and the rest head out the following day." He glanced at Bagley; I want the men staged here," he stabbed Bagley's map, "one-hour before dark."

Bagley said, "We'll leave here around noon."

"Put two scouts on point," said Wade, "you can't allow yourselves to be discovered—understood?"

As one, they all stood erect signaling that the meeting was finished. Fox spread his arms and stretched followed by a yawn. He looked at Matt with a crooked smile. "OK, then, let's get our supplies sorted before we call it a night."

Matt and Fox walked across the street and went through the supplies picking and choosing what they thought a well-stocked trader would have in their possession. After an hour, they finished. "I hope we're doing the right thing," said Matt. "Mr. Fox, you've fought alongside Duncan—do you think he'll approve of what we're doing?"

Fox saw the young man's uncertainty painfully etched across Matt's face. He reached out and placed a consoling hand on his shoulder. "If it's the correct tactical move, then yes, he'd agree." The worry began to drain from Matt's face. "He wouldn't have left you in command, unless he had confidence in you."

"I guess you're right, Mr. Fox; thanks for saying that, I'll sleep better."

Chapter 14

Concern shone in the healer's ice-blue eyes. "He's lost a lot blood," said Rebecca. She placed her pale slender hand on Farmer's forehead. "His fever is high, and he shouldn't be moved for at least a week—longer would be better."

Duncan stared at his friend, who lay delirious on the healer's table. "The bullet is out and the bleeding stopped so if he had to, could he travel?"

The tallish healer placed her fists on narrow hips; her jaw clenched, and her blonde brow furrowed. "You're not listening to me. Your friend's wound is serious; he would have bled to death if not for your prompt first-aid." She glanced at Morgan, who smiled, which further disgruntle her demeanor. "Even if you carried your friend in a wagon—just one bump too many, and all my work will have been for nothing. Now tell me—what's worth that kind of risk?"

Duncan glanced at Morgan and saw his smile, and it confused him. Ignoring Morgan for the present, he turned back to the healer. "The men who shot him may try to finish him. We need to leave, so he should go with us for his protection."

"That's ridiculous—he'll be protected while he's under my care. We're not some barbaric—"

"I think she has a point, Duncan," interrupted Morgan, who spoke to Duncan, but still smiled at Rebecca. "I'll come back in a week, or so and check on Farmer and make sure he gets home."

When Duncan started to respond, he noticed that Rebecca and Morgan were smiling at each other totally ignoring him. "Oh all right—if you think it's best. Let get something to eat and find a place to stay the night. We should get an early start."

One last look at Farmer and Duncan headed for the door. When he turned to speak to Morgan, he wasn't there. Duncan halted and turned back to Rebecca's infirmary; Morgan and she stood close engaged in a quiet conversation. As he stepped into the room, Rebecca laughed and Morgan beamed; it was obvious, he was smitten.

"Sorry to interrupt, Morgan, but—"

When Morgan turned in his direction, he didn't

seem to recognize Duncan for a split-second, and then …. "Ah, Duncan, yes, yes—food and shelter; leave early." He looked at Rebecca, would you care to join us for a late supper, or—"

"I've already eaten, but I'll join you. A hot cup of tea sounds nice. There's a place a few doors down."

She led them to a small mid-twentieth century house which the owners converted into a restaurant. Upon entering, Duncan's mouth began watering and his stomach growled. "It smells wonderful, Rebecca."

The proprietor, who looked Italian, stepped forward. Miss Rebecca, what can I do for you?" He glanced at Duncan and Morgan, he and added, "And for your friends."

She smiled at the stout proprietor, who ran his fingers through his thinning hair. It was plain to Duncan that Morgan had competition for Rebecca's attention. "Angel, this is Morgan Hayes and his friend Josh Duncan; they've been on the trail and had an accident, and could use a good meal, so I brought them to you—I'll have tea please."

"Of course, Rebecca, if they're friends of yours, then I'll feed them like family." He smiled at Duncan obviously seeing his youth as of no consequence, but at Morgan, he scowled. If Morgan noticed, he didn't respond. "Please follow me, Gentlemen."

Angel led, followed by Duncan, Rebecca, and Morgan came up the rear. Their heights neatly stepped like a row of ducks in reverse as they twisted and turned between the tables to a large one with six chairs. He seated Rebecca across from Morgan and Duncan, and then disappeared into the kitchen. When he returned, Angel's apron was replaced with a jacket, and he sat next to Rebecca. "I've taken the liberty of placing an order for you."

Soon the food began to appear. They started with pasta covered with a pesto sauce. The entrée consisted of sliced pork with a mushroom glaze, seasoned potatoes quartered and backed, and green beans. By any standard, it was a feast both in quantity and quality. Duncan pushed his plate away with a groan. "Angel, I can't remember when I've eaten so well. Thank you."

The restaurateur grinned. Duncan saw that his upper back teeth were missing making the grin resemble that of a horse. "I'm pleased to hear you like my cooking, Mr. Duncan."

"Just call me Duncan if you don't mind. I'm not comfortable with the mister part. Maybe in a few more years," he said and chuckled. "I've always felt mister was reserved for venerable old men like Mr. Hayes here." He slapped Morgan across the back.

Morgan glared at Duncan. "Keep it up, Junior, and I'll show you just how quick this venerable old man whips your butt." He glanced at Rebecca, and when he saw her fearful expression, he smiled and punched Duncan's arm to show he teased.

However, the force of the punch jolted Duncan's muscular frame. It drove home the message that he was on thin ice, and he was not to make further jokes at Morgan's expense; Duncan grinned.

Duncan and Morgan decided to sleep in the compound's stable with their animals. "It's as good a choice as any," said Morgan, who was in high spirits, and also uncharacteristically talkative. His subject matter was Rebecca: her stature, the paleness of her blue eyes, the way she carried herself, and of course her compassion and talents as a healer.

Soon, it became clear to Duncan that Morgan didn't expect a conversation; he wanted to talk about Rebecca. Duncan lost track of what Morgan said and began to think about Mary and how would he ever find her. Those thoughts led him to think of Lucky and with that a veil of sadness draped over his mind, and he felt an ache in his chest. Until now, he'd not been aware of just how much a friend and companion Lucky was.

The animals stirring at first light woke them. Duncan rose and stretched to relief his achy muscles. Morgan followed, but just groaned and complained of their accommodations. "We should've found some beds somewhere—I'm stiff as a board."

A glint of humor came to Duncan's eyes. "You seem pretty spry last night when you were courting Rebecca."

Morgan scowled as expected, but his eyes also twinkled with mirth. "I hate that Farmer got shot, but—"

"You wouldn't have met Rebecca," interrupted Duncan followed with a chuckle. "You were quick to volunteer to come back and help Farmer return home. Have you other ideas that include Rebecca?"

Pleasantness softened Morgan's normal stern expression. "I'll admit to wanting to pursue further conversation with her. If it wasn't for you and Kimball, I'd stay on for a while." The mention of Kimball's name sobered them both. "What's next, Duncan?"

"Let's find some coffee first—then we can talk." Duncan led the way back to Rebecca's infirmary. When they came in, Farmer was awake, sitting up, and Rebecca spoon fed him broth.

She wore the same clothes as the night before and looked tired. "You set up with him all night?" asked Morgan.

A ready smile curved her mouth showing straight white teeth. "I dozed over there," she pointed to a venue that contained a reading lamp, comfortable chair, and a cot. "It's not too bad; I just wouldn't want to live here."

"How is Farmer doing?" asked Duncan.

"I can hear you," said Farmer. "I'm doing find thank you. A couple of days and I'll be ready to ride."

"Unless you define a couple as seven to ten-days, you're not going anywhere," said Rebecca as her fists moved to her hips.

"She right," agreed Duncan. "You lost a lot of blood and the wound is pretty serious. Take it easy for a while; Morgan's volunteered to come back and escort you home." Duncan winked and turned to look at Rebecca.

She and Morgan had moved to the sleeping cot and fallen into a quiet conversation. "Oh," said Farmer. "Well, we all end up there eventually." He and Duncan both grinned as Rebecca and Morgan were oblivious to the comment.

"Excuse me, Rebecca," said Duncan. "Is there a place to find coffee this time of morning?"

A little startled, she looked up at him and said, "Huh! Yes in the next room—it's fresh; I just finished brewing it."

Duncan stepped into the next room and returned with two cups of coffee. Handing one to Morgan, he said, "I guess we should decide what to do about Kimball and finding Mary."

Rebecca looked at Morgan, her question shone on her face.

He tried to smile reassuringly, but failed. "Morgan?" she asked.

He sighed and shrugged his shoulders. "We weren't actually ambushed, though Farmer was—" Morgan looked at Duncan.

"It's my problem, Rebecca. Morgan and Farmer are helping find my fiancée, Mary Evans. She and her sisters—" Twenty-minutes passed and Rebecca had the complete story.

"So you think Kimball will be coming after you?" she asked.

"I don't doubt it," said Duncan. "I've stolen his brides, taken his right arm, and caused the death of his most loyal personal guard."

"Well, when you condense it like that, I guess he would be motivated to take revenge of some sort," said Rebecca.

Farmer said, "You can see now why I should go. Those men are pure trouble, and I'd hate for them to come here lookin' for revenge."

Rebecca's eyes flashed. "You'll do no such thing. Our compound has dealt with trouble before and can certainly do so now. I'll alert the council, so they can be ready." She looked to each daring them to argue. "All right then—it's settled and there's to be no more talk about it." Just as quickly as she angered, her face softened and she smiled.

"Besides," said Duncan staring at Rebecca "If Farmer leaves, Morgan won't have an excuse to return. He noticed as her cheeks reddened and she looked down at the floor. Morgan scowled, but there was no anger in his eyes.

Morgan rose and moved to stand by Farmer. "We'll be headin' out soon as we eat and pack our gear. I'll be back in ten-days or less." He glanced at Rebecca. "You take care of things—"

Farmer nodded. "I'd feel better if you'd put my gear alongside my bed—just in case."

Duncan heard the comment, and said, "We put

everything in that cupboard last night." He gestured to the vertical piece of wooden furniture standing next to his bed. Morgan opened the doors, retrieved Farmer's gun belt, and laid it on the bed. Farmer slipped them under the covers before Rebecca saw what'd happened.

"Well, if you're goin', you better get to it," said Farmer.

Duncan and Morgan shook his hand and left the room. Rebecca smiled at Farmer, and said, "I'll return soon. I want to see them off safely."

A huge toothy grin slowly spread across Farmer's face. There was no hiding the twinkle in his eyes. "Sure thing, Rebecca; and you should know Morgan's a good man, a man of means too."

Rebecca did not turn away from Farmer's grin, nor did she blush. Rather, her expression was of shrewdness. "Thank you, Farmer. That's good to know—I'm sure there are other things you can tell me about Morgan Hayes."

Farmer's grin faded. Maybe his condition wasn't as bad as she made out after all. His grin returned changing to laughter.

It was still early when Duncan and Morgan rode through Farmington's gate headed north on highway

15. After their breakfast, Rebecca stayed with them while they readied, and walked with them to the gate.

Morgan halted briefly and turned; seeing her watching, he waved. He set his horse to a gallop passing Duncan, who followed suit. Out of sight of the compound, they slowed to a walk.

"It appears," said Duncan, "that Rebecca has an interest in you, Morgan."

"I certainly hope so—I think I'm goin' to marry that woman."

***

The gates of Riverdale grew as they rode. As they passed, one of the guards waved; Duncan halted. "You know," said Duncan, "we just assumed that it was Kimball who found Mary and we rushed away without asking questions." They stared at the guards for several seconds. "Let's go—" Duncan turned Buck and led the way to the gates.

"Good day, Travelers," said the guard who waved. "What's your business in Riverdale?" His smile was friendly and inviting.

"Nothing inside thank you," said Duncan. "But some information if you please. Were you on guard yesterday morning?"

The guard squinted at Duncan. "I remember you,

you were after Kimball and men—where's the third man?"

Duncan ignored the question and asked his own, "Did you happen to notice a young blonde woman passing by yesterday morning?"

"Well," began the guard, and then he turned to his partner. "You were here too. Remember Joseph Smith?"

The other guard; older and sullen rubbed his chin and stared off into the distance trying to retrieve the requested information. Finally, he said, "Yeah, I do. Smith had a young blonde girl with him. I remember wondering how he managed to attract someone so pretty."

"Why do you say that?" asked Morgan.

The first guard answered, "You'd have to know Smith to understand. He's not very sociable— especially with women."

Duncan nudged Buck forward causing the guard to step back. "What does that mean—'especially with women'?"

The guard looked up at Duncan and seeing the level of urgency displayed in his expression, rushed to answer, "He wouldn't hurt her, or anything—its women don't tend to take to him; that's all."

Morgan inched forward and touched Duncan's arm. Duncan snapped his head around. "Take it easy, Duncan. We'll get better information if you're threating them."

Duncan looked back and surveyed the situation. Seeing that he'd shown aggression, he said, "She's my fiancée, and she was taken—" He reined Buck a few steps backward and forcing himself to be civil, he asked, "Can you please tell me the direction they traveled when they rode passed?"

The first guard pointed, and said, "South on the 84—"

Chapter 15

They turned their mounts and rode away from the Riverdale gate. The guards looked on as they reined in out of ear shot to discuss their predicament. "What do you think is going on," asked Morgan?

"It could be anyone of several options," said Duncan. "The thing is: I keep going to the bad ones."

"List 'em and we'll deal with 'em one at a time."

"Well, this Smith character might have kidnapped Mary and—"

"What's next?"

"Or, he could be trying to return her to Kimball for a reward."

"That sounds more likely, since sociably being around women is supposed to intimidate him. What else comes to mind?"

"She could have talked him into helping her return to New Lovelock—she can be pretty persuasive when she wants." Duncan smiled. It was a gentle smile as might be given to a cherished one and his eyes focused on a past memory.

"Regardless, they're headed south on the 84," said Morgan. "I suggest we search both sides and meet up just north of Henefer if we don't find them, and make our next decision then."

"What about Kimball," asked Duncan? He turned in his saddle and scanned their back trail. "The best we can hope for is a day's lead probably more like a half-day."

"If he rendezvoused with his other men, he'll have close to a dozen men. That's long odds even for us—"

Duncan returned his attention to the conversation; his smile turned cold and humorless. "You talk as if I plan to meet him head on. I plan to assassinate him from a distance. Less people will get hurt that way."

Morgan's brow pinched as he studied Duncan's face. "You don't think his men will come after us for killing Kimball?"

"No, I don't—maybe his initial group might have been so inclined, but not this bunch. They're strictly mercenaries riding for the money. Oh, we may have to deal with one or two when I kill him, but I'm sure they'll call it quits thereafter."

"Remind me not to get on your bad side," said Morgan The chuckle that followed carried no humor. "I'll take the northbound road." Morgan put heels to his mount and loped away. Duncan watched him ride off, and then reined Buck onto the southbound road toward Henefer. He rode with the hope that he would find Mary before Kimball.

***

Eliot waited with Kimball where they camped the night before. The others searched for the second party waiting somewhere on highway 80 where the 15 intersects. It was late afternoon when they returned. Kimball stood and held up his hand in greeting as they rode in. "Ah, my children have returned." Kimball's voice began to rise. "Now, I can make that defiler—that heathen pay for his indiscretions toward me, me who is God's own messenger." Eliot exchanged glances with several of the men.

Kimball marched to his horse with purpose. Eliot had to rush to keep up; he helped Leader onto his mount, and then hurried to his own. The men fell in behind Kimball and Eliot, and they led them from the camp at the gallop.

When they reached Farmington, they found Rebecca standing with the guards above the gates, which were closed.

Kimball halted; his men formed a semicircle around him. He scanned the faces of the people looking down and settled on the woman as being in command. "I am John Kimball the leader of the Henefer Compound. Why are your gates closed to me?"

Rebecca stared back. We know who you are Kimball and what you are about. Neither the girl, nor the man you seek is here."

"And I'm expected to accept your word?"

"You can believe what you will, but Duncan rode out early this morning headed north. Now move on, you are not welcome here."

One of those rare moments of sanity came to Kimball. So, he thought, she knows about the Evans girls, and Mr. Duncan. There's nothing to gain having a confrontation. He finger-combed his stringy hair and straightened in the saddle. "As you wish—" He abruptly reined his mount and galloped off northward.

***

Matt Wade sat his mount waiting for Dan Fox,

who dragged himself outside. Fox stooped forward rubbing his lower back; seeing young Wade, he sighed, "A man my age deserves a decent bed to sleep on. Too much more of this and I'll be permanently crippled."

"Aw come on, Mr. Fox," said Wade, his good humor shone on his face. You get around fine; you're just not used to riding is all. Why, another couple of weeks and you'll start to like it."

Fox loured, and then shook his head. Seeing the smile on Matt's face, he laughed aloud, and responded, "Sounds like the opinion of the young and inexperienced to me."

Hours later, riding in the northbound lane alert for other travelers, Matt raised his hand for Fox to halt.

"What is it," whispered Fox?

"Riders coming; let's duck into the trees—" Matt led the way and soon they were lost in the shadows of the tall pines. They dismounted and to steady their horses. They were downwind, Matt said, "Cover his muzzle so he won't neigh."

As they watched, a man and a young woman came into view. "It must be the couple Bagley told us about," said Wade. He didn't consider them a threat, so he looked away and tended to his horse.

As they were passing, Fox asked, "Are all the young women here-abouts fair, blonde, and blued eyed?"

Matt looked up. "Well, I'll be—" Without explanation, he swung onto his horse and bolted from the trees. "Hold up," he called!"

Startled, Mary's horse reared; throwing her butt first onto the roadway. Her only saving grace; it was a section of the road absent the concrete pavement. Joseph's mount bucked and then took flight for several hundred feet before regaining control.

As his horse skidded to a halt, Matt leapt from the saddle. Mary appeared dazed. "Mary, Mary, it's me Matt Wade. Are you hurt?"

Mary turned her face towards the familiar voice and when her eyes focus, she threw her arms around Matt's neck. "Matt, is it really you? I can't believe you found me—Duncan?"

"He's out looking for you too—can you stand?" Matt tugged her up and watched as she brushed off the grass and looked for injuries.

Fox rode up to watch the scene. "I take it this is Duncan's Mary Evans?" He glanced up the road and saw her companion waiting. "Who's the fellow with you, Miss Evans?"

Mary and Matt looked in the direction Fox nodded to. "His name is Joseph Smith, and he's trying to get me back to New Lovelock." She stepped clear of Fox and Wade. "Joseph, come back. It's OK—they're friends from New Lovelock."

They watched as Joseph considered. Finally, he nudged his mount forward and rode back. He halted, but didn't dismount. "Mary—"

"Joseph, this is Matt Wade," said Mary. "I told you about him; he's a captain of the militia at home." She turned to Matt. "Matt, this is Joseph Smith. He helped me get away from Kimball and his men at Riverdale. I promised him if he helped me get home that New Lovelock would assist him with starting over."

Smiling, Matt approached Joseph and offered his hand. "I can't speak for the whole community, but I'll do everything I can to help and know that goes for Marcus and Martha—they're important folks in New Lovelock and carry a lot of weight. You'll do fine—"

Joseph swallowed, and then licked his lips. His wide eyed stare relaxed and slowly a smile spread across his face. "This worked out just like you said, Mary. We'd find Mr. Wade, and we wouldn't have to ride all alone to your town—it's wonderful."

Matt turned to Mary, his eyes held questions. She said, "It's so great to see you—we'll talk later, but where are the rest of the militia—surely you brought more men?"

"They'll be here tomorrow—rather they'll be at the Henefer exit tomorrow." He paused to contemplate their location. "Let's mount up and I'll explain as we ride." Mary and Matt led off.

By the time, they reached the exit overpass, Mary knew as much as he about Duncan his search for her. She felt mixed emotions; she was thrilled that Duncan would go to such lengths to rescue her, but she worried about the danger it put him and his friends in. Was she really worth that much trouble? She committed to herself that she would.

Under the overpass, Matt built a small fire next to one of the columns that supported the road above and prepared coffee. Mary soon had their stores exposed and began fixing something to eat. She couldn't remember the last time she felt this good. She was rescued; Duncan had returned from California … she hummed.

After their meal, they sat watching the small fire and talked. Mary dominated the conversation with questions about Duncan. Finally, Matt said, "Mary, Duncan is fine; I'm sure. Let's talk about something else." He gave his attention to Joseph. "What skills, or interests do you have Mr. Smith?"

Joseph, who sat away from the others and withdrawn into his shell; he didn't hear Matt's question. Mary intervened. "Joseph, didn't you hear Matt asked you a question?"

When Joseph looked up, his expression was blank. His eyes blinked and he said, "Huh, were you saying something, Mary?"

"It was me, Mr. Smith. I asked if you had any special skills, or interest that would help you get along in New Lovelock."

He considered the question for a time before he answered, "Not really, Captain Wade. I lived at home with my mother and worked part-time at the trading post."

"Well, there you go—we've got several businesses that can use the kind of skill. I'm sure we'll get started off on the right foot."

Since their meeting, Fox kept a close eye on Joseph. It occurred to him that young Mr. Smith might have social issues. He asked, "Joseph, if I may call you that, how'd you and Mary meet?"

Joseph smiled at Fox. "Please do call me Joseph, Sir." He glanced at Mary, who smiled and waited patiently for him to tell his story. It occurred to him that maybe, he shouldn't tell everything. "Well, Sir—"

"Call me Dan, or Fox, Joseph," interjected Dan.

"Well, Dan, when Brother Kimball arrived, he made a big thing as how Mary was probably hiding nearby and scared to come into the compound and ask for help. I was part of the search party sent out to see if Mary was there, and she was. She was inside a camouflaged shelter. You couldn't see it until you were standing right next to it, it was something. Anyway, I didn't like the looks of Kimball, or the way he talked, so—"

"He didn't give me away and he left me water. The next morning after Kimball left, Joseph came back and offered to help me."

Fox saw Joseph turn away refusing to make eye contact with Mary; Fox wondered, what is he hiding? "That was very nice of you, Joseph. I'm sure she is grateful, and I know her fiancé will be too."

Joseph continued to stared down. "Yeah, Mary told me about him."

Wade looked at the sky. "Dan, it's about time we

made our move." He kicked dirt onto the fire to smother it without causing smoke. "We don't want them to see the smoke; it wouldn't do for them to become suspicious."

Mary handed Fox a slip of paper. "Here's the list of people I think are safe for you to speak with." She paled a bit. "Please don't tell them that I'm close by."

Fox took the list and squeezed her hand. "Don't worry, Mary. It'll be fine. Hopefully this time tomorrow the others will be here and there's no way anyone will harm you."

***

Wade and Fox halted outside the Henefer gates. "Howdy, Brothers, we're making our way home to Brigham City and hope to spent the night and maybe do some trading."

"We don't have accommodations for travelers," said one of the guards. He seemed in command.

"Brother, where's your hospitality for fellow Mormons? We're not picky; we'll sleep in a stable, so long as it's warm and dry."

The guards talked among themselves for several minutes. Finally the one in charge said, "You can stay at the main stable. The blacksmith's hearth burns night and day, so it's warm enough. Put your animals in the corral and spread your wares on the ground by the barn—fair enough?"

"Fair enough, Brother, and God bless you." After a few minutes of waiting the gates opened.

The guard in command introduced himself, "I'm Randal Banks—folks just call me Banks."

"Pleasure to meet you, Brother, I'm Matt Wade and this is Daniel Fox." They shook hands in turn. Where's the stable?" asked Matt.

"Down the street and turn right at the corner, you can't miss it. There's space at the blacksmith's, you can bed down there."

"Where can we setup for trading?" asked Matt.

"Out front of the blacksmith's place, I reckon, he's not workin' this late. Word 'll get 'round by the time you're ready," said Banks.

They followed the street as instructed and found the stable easily, after putting their animals into the corral they focused on setting up shop for trade. As predicted, people began to gather before they'd finish laying out their trade goods.

Henefer was not a prosperous compound. Their farming appeared to consist of large gardens inside the walls. The vegetables canned in glass jars and carefully wrapped were of the greatest interested to the people of the compound; followed by the fruits and jams. The few pieces of hardware they'd collected from the men at camp were also welcomed.

As the people came forward, Matt introduced himself and tried to solicit their names. Fox held back and checked Mary's list for people safe to talk to. The compound's inhabitants were fearful and closed mouth. Only a few responded with their names.

Finally, one young woman, who strongly resembled Mary, approached. "Hello, I'm Matthew Wade—see anything of interest?"

The young woman smiled. "I'm Mrs. Sharon Kimball, pleased to me you, too. We don't get many traders stopping by."

It was subtle, but Matt caught the nod that Fox gave. "If you please, Sister Kimball, there are some special items over here by Brother Fox." He touched her elbow and guided her to Fox.

Away from the others, Fox decided to gamble. He turned his back to the gathering and stood next to Sharon. "We're friends of Mary Evan's," he whispered.

Sharon couldn't have reacted more strongly than if she been struck. She gasped and snapped her head around to stare at Dan Fox. He reached out and grabbed her arm to steadier her. Finally, Sharon regained her composure. "So she made it then?"

"Yes, she is safe and with friends." He exaggerated.

"Then why are you here?"

"To help, if you and the compound will allow it."

Her brow wrinkled, and her eyes gave him a piecing stare; she searched for the truth of his statement. Then she quickly looked around to insure no one could hear. "What do you mean help?"

Dan smiled trying to reassure her. "Just what I said—" He too glanced about to insure their privacy. "Kimball and a dozen of his guards are away. How many guards are left—maybe another ten to twenty? We have more men than that standing by."

"How does that help us with you outside and the guards inside?"

She's a shrewd, thought Fox. "That's the problem. If we can get word to enough people on the inside that we're here to help, and for them not to throw in with the guards; then we can sneak in and take them without a fight."

Fox looked on patiently as Sharon considered the proposition. It was a huge risk for her if the attempt failed and she was found out. Finally, she said, "I have a two-year old daughter—"

Dan saw the concern in her eyes. "—and?"

"There aren't many people who would trust me. I'm a Kimball wife and not allowed outside his enclave that often, especially when he's here. Where would I start," asked Sharon?

He offered a folded piece of paper, and asked, "Do you know these people? You could start with them—"

Sharon scanned the list. "I know them, or know of them, but—"

"Just speak to them and tell them Mary's story, and that we'll help them rid themselves of Kimball."

"What's to become of us?" Sharon's expression seemed to wilt.

The question caused Fox to pause. After a few seconds, he said, " I guess it depends on how the rest of the community sees you—victim, or elitist, which seems doubtful. What would do?"

Sharon only nodded as she considered her situation. Then, she asked, "What about the people that believe Kimball is a prophet?"

"If they can't be persuaded, my guess is they'd be exiled."

Her eyes went wide. "What of Kimball? If he

remains alive there will always be a threat against us."

Fox didn't look away, but his expression sobered. "That subject has been resolved— regardless if the people join us or not."

Sharon straightened and tucked the list into her pocket. "I've a few hours yet before I must return. I will set thing in motion, but how will you know?"

"Can you get someone to contact us before we leave?"

"If I'm successful, someone will come, if not—"

"Fair enough," said Fox and he watched as she departed and walked toward the houses beyond her enclave. The di is cast, he thought, nothing to do now but wait.

Of all those who came to trade few gave their name and only Sharon's name appeared on the Mary's list. It was late, so Matt and Fox rolled up their supplies and moved into the barn. Sitting next to their fire, they ate their meager meal and drank coffee. They quietly talked about the day's events.

"What do you think will happen, Mr. Fox?"

Dan Fox glanced at his companion. "The guards haven't arrived to take us prisoner, so I guess thing might work out."

At Fox's comment, Wade startled and began to look around as if danger was imminent. "I hadn't thought about that—should we take turns standing guard?"

A chuckled was Fox's first response. "If we were in danger, I suspect we'd already know it and be trussed up somewhere waiting for Kimball's return and some unpleasant questioning."

Though Fox couldn't see, Wade blushed embarrassed by his naive behavior. "Well, just the same we should take turns sleeping, so we'll be awake if we have a guest."

Fox nodded. "You go ahead and turn in, Matt. I'm not sleepy yet."

Chapter 16

Relieved by Wade, Fox now stood his second turn on watch; his watched showed 4:00 A.M. He was ready to wake young Matt to spell him, when the barn door creaked. He stayed in the shadows and watched as the door swung ajar far enough to allow a person to enter. The starlight blinked out for just second; someone was in the barn. As they stole toward where he and Matt were expected to sleep, Fox waited for them to pass his position. The figure was slight; a woman? "May I help you," said Fox.

The figure whirled with a hand over her mouth to stifle a scream. "Oh, it's you—you scared me," said Sharon Kimball.

Fox left the shadows and stepped closer to be heard. "I didn't expect to see you again. Won't you be missed?"

"So long as Leader is away, I'm in no danger, but

I'll need your help getting back into the house."

"I'm sure we can work something out—let's wake Wade." She followed him to the hay stack where they'd spread their bedrolls. Fox tapped Wade's foot with his own. "Wade, we've got company."

Wade startled and sat upright. "What?"

"Easy, Wade—Sharon Kimball has returned."

Matt rose to stand with them. "What time is it?"

"A little after four," said Fox. "You awake enough yet to listen and remember?" He watched as Wade yawned, shook himself and then vigorously rubbed his face.

"Sure—go ahead—shoot."

Sharon stepped closer. Though she was in the barn with no one else to hear, she still spoke softly, "I've spoken to several families, who I believe speak for several. They're with us, provided Kimball is permanently removed from the compound."

"Do you mean executed," asked Fox?

Sharon didn't immediately respond, at length, she said. "Yes, but away from here if that's possible."

"It will be arranged, Ma'am," said Wade.

"So how many of the compound will side with us," asked Fox?

"Most, but there are some who believe in

Kimball; they won't fight, but they won't cooperate and will warm the guard if they learn of what's about to happen."

"How many of the guards are loyal to Kimball," asked Matt.

"The six who guard the house; those at the gate and elsewhere are family men and are volunteers—they'll be with us," said Sharon.

Fox asked, "Do they keep you in or others out?"

Sharon gave a humorless laugh. "A little of both, I suppose, but mostly to keep us inside the enclave, so we can't speak to others."

Matt asked, "So you and your families may be in danger?"

"Not from the guards directly, but if you try to take the enclave then some of us could get hurt in the fighting."

"Would it be possible to get all of you in one place, so we can get you out to safety," asked Matt. He paused to consider. "Better yet, could we sneak several men inside and take them by surprise?"

Sharon was warming to the ideal of escaping the enclave. Her voice rose and when she spoke it held conviction. "I don't see why we can't do both. There is a tree with a low branch outside Judith's bedroom window. That's how I got out. You can bring your men in that way and then help us escape."

Fox's expression conveyed doubt. "You're sure all the wives are OK with this?" He squinted in the dark to see her face.

"Well, we haven't spoken to everyone yet, but—"

Fox couldn't make out the features of her face, but he heard something in her voice. "Out with it— what aren't you telling us?"

There was hesitation, finally, she said, "Judith and I have talked and agreed this is best. Ann and Beth, Leader's first two wives, are unaware of what's going on—they're older, so he doesn't bother them anymore." She sighed and added, "They don't have children."

"Old," asked Fox?

Sharon smiled sheepishly. "They're not as old as you Mr. Fox. Ann's thirty-five, Beth's thirty, Judith is twenty-five, and I'm twenty. Leader likes younger wives."

"How will you get them into your room," asked Wade. He grinned at Fox. "They're not infirmed are they?" Fox scowled.

"Judith has the strongest personality. If she tells them to come to her room they will. They'll just assume it's a wives meeting. If you can have your men inside before they arrive—"

"Sounds risky," said Wade. "If they called out the guards might hear and come to investigate."

"That's doubtful, Mr. Wade. Our quarters are upstairs and away from the areas where the guards stay." She paused and looked down at her feet; her voice got smaller. "Sometimes, we have—um disagreements. The guards won't come even if the wives do shout."

"Never understood why a man felt the need for more 'n one wife," said Fox. "I got my hands full with just one."

Sharon looked up and regaining her voice said, "It's not at all like that, Mr. Fox. We're more like sisters, and sometimes sister have disagreements. For the most part we get along just fine."

Fox held up his hands. "All I'm saying is one's enough for me."

Wade spoke up, "Now that's settled let's make our plans." He looked from one to the other; sure that he had their attention, he continued. "Can you get the other wives to Judith's room at nine sharp tomorrow night?" Sharon nodded. "We'll come over the wall at eight-thirty behind the temple. From there four men will come to the enclave and enter Judith's room before nine."

"What if there's a trap," asked Fox, who stared at Sharon? His express hard and menacing.

Wade also stared at Sharon, but she did not look away. "We'll leave our men outside the wall until we've received a signal that all is safe; then we'll swarm the compound and surround the enclave."

***

Mary awoke at first light and started a fire for coffee and breakfast. Joseph roused at the smell of food cooking. "Ugh, I'm so tired of sleeping on the ground—it's cold and damp. How do you stand to live like this?"

Shaking her head, Mary said, "You'll feel better after you've had something to eat—here's a hot cup of coffee to warm you."

Joseph crouched by the fire and warmed his hands before taking the coffee. "When do you expect your friends to return?"

In answer to his question, they heard horses cross over head. "Any minute now," she said. A few minutes later, Wade rode into camp followed by Fox. "Good morning—coffee?" she asked.

"None for me thanks," said Fox. "I need to get a

few hours of sleep—it was a long night."

Wade smiled at his new friend and then walked to the fire. "I'll have a cup and then see to the horses." Fox waved dismissively and looked for a place to roll out his bedding.

An hour before dark, Bernie and the remainder of the men joined Mary, Matt, Fox, and Joseph Smith beneath the overpass. They were twenty-five strong and anxious to have the nights work behind them.

Bernie dismounted and approached Mary giving her a huge grin. Holding by the shoulders inspecting, he said, "I can see why Duncan wants you back. You're the prettiest girl I've seen, except for my Lisa."

Mary's face reddened, but her smile said she liked the compliment. "You have to be Bernie Olsson; you couldn't be anyone else. Duncan's told me so much about you and Lisa; I would've known you anywhere."

"And I you—"

There were several small fires for brewing coffee and the preparation of food. Soon everyone was fed, and settled down to listen to Matt and Dan Fox. "Here's the plan," said Wade. "I'll take six-men over the wall with me at eight-thirty. Two will remain to guard the wall while the rest of us secure Kimball's."

Fox stepped up. "We'll need six-ladders to scale the wall. Once, we've received Wade's signal the rest of will breach the wall and swarm the compound."

"What about the people?" asked Bernie.

"Most of them will be with us—we'll be on guard, but if this goes as planned no one gets hurt," said Wade. "Stealth and surprise are critical, so keep that in mind while we're out here preparing for our attack." He scanned their faces making eye contact with each. "Are there any more questions?"

No one spoke. "OK, then," said Fox, "let's get to it." He and the others moved away from the fire.

Wade assigned Bagley and Young to stand watch at each end of the overpass. The rest broke into four groups and fashioned there ladders. Tank Shaw and Bernie formed one group; they looked at each other. Tank said, "We'll need good sized saplings to hold us."

Bernie nodded and smiled. "—and one-at-a-time on the ladder, too." The rest of their group laughed.

Nearby, Wade hissed, "Keep it down, Men, they'll hear you."

Their faces sobered for just an instant, and then they snickered under their breaths; more from nervousness than humor. In less than an hour, they'd cut and fashioned four-ladders to breach the wall. They broke up into groups and moved out among the trees to wait.

At 8:00, Wade with six-men struck out using the silhouette of the temple's steeple as a beacon. Wade was first over the wall and pleasantly surprised to find crates stacked forming a makeshift stairway. The men followed; they headed for the enclave.

At 8:30, they were beneath the tree where Wade helped Sharon gain reentry into the house. There was no light from the window ... was it a trap? At his signal, two-men hoisted Wade into the tree. He climbed to the window and waited. After what seemed like hours, the window opened slowly; Sharon stuck her head out and looked around. "Come in quickly," she said. Wade waved to his men.

Within minutes, they all stood in the center of the room. A matched flared revealing Judith's present as she lit an oil lamp. Wade scanned the room's occupants. In addition to Sharon and Judith, there were their children. "Get the other two," said Wade.

Sharon and Judith instructed their children, and then left the room. Wade and his men did their best to conceal themselves from view from the doorway. Conversation came from the hallway. "—why do we have to talk this late? Can't it wait 'til in the morning?" The door swung open and Sharon pushed the woman inside. "Sharon, what are you—" She froze when she saw the men.

As she prepared to scream, one of the men stepped up from behind and clamped his hand over her mouth as he dragged her away from the door. The door opened a second time and the scene repeated with Judith pushing the other wife into the room.

Ann and Beth struggled, but were held tight. Finally, Judith raised her hand and they stopped. She looked at each; her expression was firm maybe even menacing. "Listen to me." They both stared at her. "They will release you if you promise to keep quiet while I explain what's happened." They nodded and the men removed their hands, but stood ready behind them.

Sharon stood next to Judith. "The members of the compound have had enough of the Leader and his tyranny. You two have been able to seal yourselves off from what's been going on, but no longer. When this is over, you'll have the choice of staying and help things to improve, or you can leave."

Both women paled and stared at Sharon wide eyed. Ann, the oldest, spoke first, "Why are you doing this Sharon. After Leader has Mary Evans, he'll leave you alone."

Sharon's eyes went to the children as her answer.

Beth stepped away from Ann to stand by Sharon. "I'm still young enough to start over—I'm with you."

Ann's nostrils flared as she jutted out her chin. Crossing her arms, she said "You'll be sorry when the Leader finds out?"

Judith moved closer to Ann. Her tone was conciliatory. "Ann, think about this for a minute—he's changed. I think he's insane and things will only get worse.—don't you see?"

Ann's jaw clinched; color flushed her neck and face, and her eyes hooded as she sneered at Judith. "What do I care about these people? Did they stand up for me when Kimball came for me? My parents, my own parents prayed with that bastard before making me leave with him. I—was—fifteen—years—old!" Her voice steadily rose. "He beat and raped me day after day. They knew, but did they do anything to stop him? Hell no, they didn't! Now you're asking me to help save them? You and they can all go to hell."

No one moved for several seconds, and then Ann collapsed on the bed sobbing uncontrollably. It was Sharon who came and held her head while she cried. "It's all right, Ann, we understand."

Wade and his men, who'd been ready to bind and gag Ann, now, looked at one another uncomfortably. Beth and Judith consoled the children; themselves about to cry.

After, ten-minutes, Ann's loud sobbing quieted to deep breaths and an occasional fit of weeping. Eventually, she sat up on the edge of the bed and stare at the group with her red puffy eyes. "I'm sorry," she said. "I'll help stop that bastard."

The awkwardness of Wade's smile made Sharon laugh. "It's unanimous—I told it would be all right."

Matt moved to the window carrying the lamp. He placed his hat in front of the lamp and then removed it. The militia leader repeated the action several times per their prearranged sequence, which signaled the all clear and for them to swarm the compound.

The ladder bowed under his weight, but Bernie insisted he would the first over the wall. Tank and Little Carl, who was not so little, followed up their respective ladders. The remainder of the men scurried over like ants and gather in the shadow of the temple.

Dan Fox, the last man over the wall joined the group. "We're all over, Bernie."

"OK," said Bernie. "We break up into four groups of five. Disburse as planned—remember: this is a peaceful takeover."

***

Wade and his men crept down the stairs to the guard room. Two men patrolled the enclave's perimeter and one man guarded its gate. There were three men in the guardroom asleep. On Matt's signal, the guards were awakened. They froze when they saw rifles pointed at their heads. "Whose in command," asked Wade?

The guard closest to the doorway spoke, "Me—"

Matt turned to the voice and saw a man not much older than he. A well-groomed blonde man extended his hands and slowly rose from his bed. "Get dressed," commanded Wade.

The guard complied and stood facing Wade. "Now what—"

Wade gestured toward the door. "Step to the front door and tell the guard at the gate to come in here."

The guard did not move. Instead, he asked, "What are you trying to accomplish? We're not a wealthy compound, nor do we have a lot of supplies. You're risking your lives for little potential of reward."

"What I'm trying to accomplish is for you tell the gate guard to come in here. If we have to go out and get him someone may unnecessarily get killed." He paused to let his words sink in and then added, "So what's it going to be?"

The guard shrugged and moved to the door. Matt was close behind. At the front door, the guard opened it and called, "Hey, Walt, I need to see you in here for a minute."

Walt responded, but Matt couldn't make out the words. "No it can't wait—it'll just take a minute," said the guard in command. He stepped back from the door as Walt entered.

Stepping into the house, he hesitated when he saw his command's hand's raised. From behind him, he heard, "Don't move." As he felt the barrel of a rifle jammed into his back. "Now close the door and put down your weapons," said Wade.

Matt, turned them both over to his men and watched through the window as the other two guards met at gate. Not seeing Walt, they halted. "Where's

Walt," asked the guard on the right? The other shrugged. First guard added, "He must be in the house with Chris."

When they turned to march to the rear of the house, they were each confronted by two men; the guards dropped their weapons and raised their hands. Bagley said, "Inside." Their guns were collected and taken in behind them.

They herded the guards into the guardroom and tied them hand and foot. James, the command guard, said, "If you're here to kidnap the Leader's wives you're making a big mistake. He'll hunt you down no matter where you go, you can't hide from him."

Matt didn't respond to James. To Bagley, he said, "Lon, you and Shumway stay here and keep an eye on them." He lowered his voice. "Regardless of what they said—don't talk to them."

"Yes, Sir," said Bagley and turned to guard his prisoners.

Wade and his men left the enclave to find Bernie and Fox to see if they needed help. He found them at the temple. The vast majority of the compound's inhabitants milled around the meeting hall talking among themselves, or to Duncan's Force, as they'd begun to call themselves. There were thirty plus people seated in the pews, each looked on stoically at the others; guarded by four men.

"Not a shot fired, or even a struggle to talk about," said Bernie as Wade walked towards him.

"Same here," said Wade. "Though, had they been given the chance there would have been a fight." Matt looked around for Fox. He spied him speaking with several men near Fox's age.

As Wade walked up to join them, he heard Fox say, "—if that's the way you want to handle it, we'll support your decision."

"Handle what?" asked Matt.

Fox turned to greet his new friend. "These men speak for the majority of the compound. We were discussing their options regarding the people who remain loyal to Kimball."

"Their solution?" asked Matt.

"Exile," said the gray-haired man next to Fox. "They're the ones that reported on us when we didn't follow Kimball's instructions." He stood tall and squared his wide shoulders. "I was for turning them out empty-handed, but I got out voted."

Fox looked at Wade and shrugged. "They've got 'til noon tomorrow to gather what they can and leave."

Matt surveyed the group. There didn't appear to be many children, which made him feel some better about the situation. He turned back to the gray haired man. "You can't come up with another solution? I mean—they've no place to go."

"It's their choice," said the gray haired man. "They could stay if they denounced Kimball, but they think he's going to save them."

Wade and Fox exchanged looks; Kimball would soon be dead.

"What if they change their minds and want to come back to their homes and resume their lives here?" asked Wade.

The old man looked at several of his peers. They came to an unspoken agreement. "If they leave—they can't come back."

"Can we speak with them and try to get them to change their minds? They don't have any idea what it's like out there."

Again, the gray-haired man exchanged glances with his peers. "Do as you please, Young Man, but it'll do you no good."

Wade and Fox moved to in front of the pews. "Maybe you should be the one to speak to them, since you're older." Fox grimaced. "Oh, I didn't mean it that way—it's just you've more experience, so they're more likely to listen to you over me. –that's all."

"Ah," said Fox. "It's good you don't think I'm old." The irony in his voice was thick as he focused his stare on the young militia captain. Then, he chuckled. "Alright, I suppose you're correct in that they're more likely to believe me than you."

"I truly meant no disrespect, Mr. Fox. I—"

"Stop digging, Son, before you get so deep, you can't crawl out." Fox then turned his attention to those seated in the pews. "Ladies and Gentlemen, please may I have your attention?" Most looked up, but some continued to stare at the floor. Fox continued, "I understand you've chosen to accept exile rather than denounce your believe in John Kimball."

They continued to stare with dull-eyed expressions; showing no interest at all. Matt stepped forward. "Please listen, we're trying to help you. Can't you see that?"

A thin dark-haired woman with angry-eyes and a shrewish manner said, "Is that why you've thrown us out of our homes—to help us?"

"That's your choice," said Fox. "We're here to free you from the tyranny of living day-to-day under John Kimball's rule. If you want to stay, then renounce your allegiance to Kimball."

At the back of the group, a man closer to Fox's age with a bit of gray at his temples stood. "May I speak?" Fox nodded. "Our allegiance to Leader Kimball isn't political. We accept that he is God's prophet; therefore, as Mormons, we have no choice."

Fox wasn't a religious man, but he did believe in a higher power and had a strong sense of right and wrong. He began to understand that what he asked was for them to renounce their faith. His shoulders slumped as he looked at Wade. "I don't have a clue as to how I should respond. It's what they believe."

Chapter 17

There were forty-people exiled from Henefer;
most were women and children. With them, they took
food, supplies, and such personal items that space
would allow. Of the eight-families, they had fourteen-
horses and three-wagons.

The man, Jed Carlson, who spoke for the group
the night before also lead them out of the compound.
As he passed through the gates, he looked neither
right, nor left, and his head was held high.

At the main highway, they headed north in hopes
of finding their lost prophet John Kimball. He would
be their salvation.

***

Southbound on highway 84, Duncan and
Morgan loped their horse intending to reach Coalville
before nightfall. They heard the exiles before they
actually saw them; they moved into the median forest

to watch their approach. "That's a sorry excuse for a wagon train," said Morgan. "They look more like refugees."

"I wonder," said Duncan. "The animals look fresh, and so do the people. They've not been on the road long at all." He nudged Buck's flanks and they walk out to meet them.

As they approached, the stern looking man in front raised his hand halting the group. He rested his hands on the pommel of his saddle and waited for Duncan and Morgan. As they reined in, he said, "We are peaceful and not looking for trouble. What is it you want from us, Brothers?

"Nor do we seek trouble, Sir," said Duncan. "We hope to secure some general information about the way south. Are the roads safe?"

Though he tried to appear relaxed, Jed's tense posture lessened as he exhaled. His expression softened as he smiled. "I'm afraid I can only speak for the distance to Henefer."

Duncan's head tilted as he studied Jed. "How's that again?"

"We've just begun our travel northward to find our leader."

Duncan and Morgan exchanged glances.

Duncan asked, "We'd heard the people never left; it wasn't allowed."

Jed smiled, and said, "It is true we are a closed community, or at least we were. With help from outsiders, we've been exiled."

Duncan bit his lower lip to suppress the elation that grew. He looked at Morgan, who smiled mildly and nodded. "I certainly hope that no one was injured."

"It was a bloodless affair. It was mostly neighbors turning against neighbors. The outsides dealt with the guards."

"Well, good luck to you and I hope a better future—we need to be moving along." Before Jed could respond, Duncan reined Buck to the side and kicked him into a gallop. Morgan followed, but at more reasonable pace. Shortly, Duncan slowed and loped along, which allowed Morgan to catch up.

"You think Bernie and Fox took the compound?" asked Morgan.

I think Matt Wade with Bernie and Dan's help captured the compound. Fox was mostly the emissary who persuaded the people inside that it was their one chance to get rid of Kimball."

As they approached the Henefer compound they

slowed to a walk. The first thing of unusual note was the gates were open. Duncan recognized Lon Begley and Elon Shumway standing guard.

As they approached, Begley stepped forward to greet them. "Sir, it is good to see you that you have fared well." He looked past Morgan. "Where is Mr. Bennett?"

"He was injured and we had to leave him with friends." Duncan grinned at Morgan as he continued. Mr. Hayes has promised to retrieve him in a week, or so. I believe he has other business there, too."

By Bagley's confused expression it was clear he didn't understand the inside joke. Morgan interjected, "Never mind—whose idea was it to capture the compound?"

Bagley came to attention and said, "Why, Captain Wade, Sir."

Duncan eyes twinkled with humor as he looked at Morgan. "I thought as much. No one hurt?"

"None, Sir—" Bagley glanced inside the compound. "There's one more thing, Sir. Your fiancée is inside, too."

"Mary is here!" Duncan sat bolt upright to see inside the compound. "Where is she—is she all right?" Excited, Duncan didn't give Bagley time to speak. "Well, speak up man, where is she?"

Morgan placed his hand on Duncan's arm. "Give him a chance to speak, Duncan." Morgan nodded to Bagley who'd stepped back.

"She's at Kimball's enclave." Bagley pointed inside.

Throwing the reins to Morgan, Duncan leapt from Buck and ran pushing his way through the people gathered near the gate. Unlike when he snuck into Kimball's house the enclave was open. He bound up the stair with excitement and banged on the door and called, "Mary—it's me Duncan—Mary are you here?"

The door swung open. Judith stood in the doorway. "Mr. Duncan, Mary is visiting your friends Mr. Fox and Mr. Olsson. They're staying in one of the exiled member's house." She stepped out on the porch and gestured. "It's three-houses down on your left."

Half-way down the steps, he jerked to a stop and reversed back toward Judith, and said, "Thank you." Then, he cleared the remaining steps with a single bound and hit the ground at a full run. As he closed on the house, he saw its front door open and Mary stepped through followed by Dan Fox. Duncan called, "Mary!"

Mary turned to the sound of the voice calling her name. Her hands came to her mouth as she gasped; then tears spilled down her face as she jumped from the porch and ran to Duncan. She nearly bowled him over as she leaped into his arms. "Duncan, it's you. I can't believe it—you found me."

She hugged his neck and kissed his face; all the while asking questions. "Are you all right—where have you been—why didn't you write—"

He scooped her up into his arms and carried back to the porch where Dan Fox and now Bernie Olsson waited. Both men grinned at young couple's display affection. Morgan followed leading Buck; he also grinned.

On the porch, he lowered her to stand; though she did not release her grip from his neck. Stooped, he shook hands with Fox and Bernie. Finally, he took Mary up into his arms and kissed full on the mouth for several seconds. When he released her, she stepped back. Her face was flush and her breathing heavy. He turned to Bernie and Dan. "We've got trouble coming. Kimball's about at best a half-day ride north of her."

Fox gazed toward the gates. "I guess we should

button things up, but we've more men and have him out gunned."

"He'll have the exiles with him," said Morgan.

"Still," said Fox, "They won't be that much help to him."

Mary had tucked herself under Duncan's arm with her arm around his waist. She looked up at him. "They're mostly women and children. Isn't there a way to avoid a fight?"

Duncan and Morgan looked at each other, and then Duncan released Mary to stand directly in front of her. Her held her at arm's length staring into her eyes, and said, "There's only one-way."

She held his gaze for several seconds and then comprehension came to her. "Oh," she said, but she didn't look away.

"Once it's done, he'll never bother you or the girls again," said Duncan. He scanned the people of the compound milling around going about their daily business. "They'll be free of him too."

"How do we proceed," asked Fox. "We'll need time to organize."

Duncan moved off the porch to meet Matt Wade marching across the road toward him. "We were concerned about you, Duncan."

They shook hands. "I guess we should have sent word somehow, but—" Duncan glanced over his shoulder at Mary, and then continued, "There just wasn't time."

A knowing smile creased Matt's face. "I understand."

Bernie, Fox and Morgan joined Duncan and Matt. Duncan placed a hand on Matt's shoulder. "Kimball and his men—most like the exiles too will be here in a matter of hours." Matt's expression sobered. Close the gates and put our men on the wall. I don't want him to see anyone he knows— except for you and me." He smiled, at his friend. "By the way, you did a good job taking the compound."

Matt's shoulders squared. "Thank you, Duncan. It means a lot to hear you say that."

Still smiling, Duncan added, "Marcus will know about it, too.

While Fox, Bernie, and Wade handled the compound's security, Mary took Duncan and Morgan into the house for food and coffee. Though she knew from Wade the reason why Duncan's return had been delayed, she didn't have the details. So as she cooked and served, she grilled her fiancé.

Morgan; curious about Mary, and also wanting to

know the details of Duncan's California adventure sat quietly and listened.

When Matt came in to report, he heard Mary asking, "—so what does Molly look like—is she pretty?"

Duncan saw Matt enter, and said, "Not now, Mary. I'll tell you about her and Sophia later." He jumped up and grabbing Matt's arms went outside.

Morgan followed and as he closed the door, they heard Mary exclaim, "Sophia—Duncan who is Sophia?"

"I would never have thought Mary could be so jealous," said Duncan as he scowled at Morgan and Matt's laughter.

Matt said, "I think its worry, Duncan. She hadn't heard from you all that time, and then Kimball's men grabbed her—"

"What's up?" asked Duncan.

"I posted Shumway where he could watch the road—he just rode in. Kimball and the exiles will be here inside an hour."

Chapter 18

Kimball flanked by his guards rode at the head of the column of exiles. He halted within eye shot of the gates. Upon recognition of Duncan, he raised his single arm and cursed, "Damn you, Duncan. You are Satan's own demon, and I will see you sent to hell."

His followers mumbled their unanimity.

Duncan smiled down at Kimball. He could see that the leader strained to keep himself in check. "Mary's here too."

Even though there was a distance between them, it wasn't so far that Duncan couldn't see the change in Kimball's face. His expression changed into rage, and he pulled at his hair. Eliot reached out to study the leader and helped him regain his composure. Sanity returned, he said, "That harlot is no longer part of God's plan for me. You may keep her. Now leave my compound!"

Continuing to smile, Duncan said, "No—these people have had enough of you and your cruel and oppressive dictatorship."

Kimball, emboldened by the many witnesses, rode closer to the gates. His face white with fury; spittle flew out as he spoke. "You can't stay in there forever. I'll be waiting when you come out."

Duncan didn't respond, he tipped his hat and stepped back out of sight from below. Kimball jerked on the reins so hard, he cut his horses mouth and it reared throwing him to the ground. The men on the wall laughed and pointed as Kimball struggled to stand. Eliot rushed to his side and helped him regain his footing.

***

"That went well—don't you think, Duncan," said Morgan, who was smiling. "You've got him so riled up, he may have a stroke, and your problem will be solved."

"I know you're going to kill him, Duncan, why didn't you do then," asked Bernie. "It would have been an easy shot for you."

"A lot of these people may want him dead, but they don't want to stand by and see him executed," said Duncan.

Wade chimed in, "According to those I've spoken to, Kimball has raped, stolen, and murdered, or least ordered it."

"Duncan's right," said Fox. "Regardless of his crimes, he's not been publicly tried and convicted. So, if Duncan to kill him now would be seen as murder—hell Kimball would become a martyr."

Bernie looked at Duncan. "So you're not going to kill him?"

Duncan stared at Morgan. "If he were to die of natural causes it would solve everyone's problem."

Morgan stopped smiling and returned Duncan's stare. "What do you have in mind? Whatever it is, it has to happen soon."

***

It was after midnight when they went over the wall behind the temple. Duncan dropped to the ground first followed by Morgan, Bernie, and Wade. Duncan had tried to dissuade Wade from coming, but he was determined, so Duncan relented.

Leading the group, Duncan circled around behind where Kimball and the exiles camped. Finding Kimball was a simple task. His tent stood in the center of the camp. The camp was asleep except for a single guard, who sat near the fire. It was obvious they hadn't considered that anyone wanted, or would leave the compound, so their guard was down.

As they watched the camp, Duncan pointed to Matt and then to a place in the tall grass. Matt staying low to the ground took his rifle and moved the location. Concealed by the tall grass, Matt took a kneeling shooting position and scanned his field of vision. Fully, half the campsite was in his line of fire. Morgan went in the opposite direction and confirmed the same for his field of vision.

"Are you sure about this, Bernie?" asked Duncan. "I think I can handle him alone." Duncan looked down and stretched the sheet of rubber cut from an old truck tire tube again insuring its flexibility.

"You'll need me, Duncan. Besides it's my chance to repay you for helping me save Lisa—I couldn't have done it without you."

"All right then, let's get on with it," said Duncan.

The guard's chin rested on his chest, and he hadn't moved for twenty-minutes, or more. His study breathing indicated he was in a deep level of sleep; it was time.

Duncan took the lead with Bernie following close behind. They paused at the back of the canvas tent to listen. Hearing nothing, he lifted the base of the tent to peer inside. Just inches away, Kimball lay on his bedroll sleeping. With only the light of the campfire to see, they circled to the front.

Untying the flaps, they crept into the tent. Kimball's face was placid without expression of any kind; he looked harmless. They lower to their hands and knees, and crawl next to where Kimball slept. As prearranged, Duncan positioned himself above Kimball's head, while Bernie stayed at his side.

Slowly, Duncan unfolded the sheet of rubber and held it poised over Kimball's face. Bernie positioned himself to pin Kimball's body. Just as Duncan said, "Now," Kimball's eyes opened full; they grew wide with recognition and then terror. There was hesitation by all as each comprehended what was happening.

Three things occurred simultaneously: Kimball gasped a breath to yell; Duncan stretched the rubber sheet over Kimball's face; and Bernie lay atop Kimball's body pinning him to the ground. Bernie's huge size confined Kimball's resistance to clawing at Bernie's arm, and jiggling his feet. No noise was made.

***

Sensing a presence in his tent, Kimball opened his eyes expecting to see Eliot. The face was familiar but who was it, and then it came to him. Duncan, the man who stole his brides, who took his arm, was here; why? He focused on the black sheet hovering over his head, and then he knew; assassination. They were here to kill him. Where was Eliot, where was the rest of his guard? Could this really be happening, or was it a nightmare? He sucked in a great breath of air to scream, and then everything went black.

He could smell the rubber; taste it. Why couldn't he move? There was a great weight on his body forcing the air from his lungs. When he tried to draw in air, there was nothing; something prevented his breathing. He struggled to get his hand to his face to clear the obstruction, but his arm wouldn't move. What happened to his body? Why wouldn't it obey him? He clawed and kicked at the unyielding entity atop him, but nothing he did allowed him to breath.

His heart pounded in his ears as he fought, but his strength rapidly began to wane; his lungs burned, and he saw large bursts of colored light in his mind's eye. He quit struggling followed by a great sense of peacefulness. In the distance, a single light grew brighter and larger as it approached, and then there was nothing. John Kimball was dead.

***

Duncan held the rubber sheet in place for five-minutes, though it seemed much longer. When Kimball stopped struggling, Bernie eased off Kimball's body. His breathing labored from the effort it took to hold Kimball still. In a whisper, Bernie asked, "Is he dead?"

After removing the rubber sheet, Duncan felt for a pulse. Finding none, he merely nodded. He smoothed Kimball's expression and adjusted his clothing. "Hand me his blanket," said Duncan. Together, Bernie and Duncan positioned Kimball as if he died peacefully in his sleep. Hopefully, they'll think he had a stroke."

Bernie nodded. "Now what?" he asked.

"We slip away without being seen." The canvas tent walls hung to the ground; he listened for several seconds before he lifted the back of the tent to check for guards. "We're clear," he said and began to crawl under. Outside, he held the canvas for Bernie, who struggled to get through the tight space. Seeing no one, they crouched and returned to the trees where Wade and Morgan waited.

Morgan looked at Duncan. His eyes held a question. Duncan nodded, and without further comment led the group back to the compound.

None of them slept; at dawn, they mounted the wall over the gate and waited for the exiles to begin their day. People began to mill about; campfires started, and breakfasts prepared. It was about 6:30 when a commotion started at the center of their camp. People crowded around a single tent, but soon walked away. Their movement without purpose, they just walked. Wails of anguish could be heard coming from the women.

Finally, Elliot came to the gate. "We need the healer," he called. "Something's wrong with the Leader—"

The gray-haired man who spoke for the elders was there and stared down at Elliot. "How do we know this isn't a trick?"

"Please, Mr. Layton, the Leader is in his tent, and he's not breathing. I'm afraid he might be dead."

"Eliot," said Layton. "You know if a man's dead or not."

"But this is the Leader—he's God's prophet—maybe he's not."

Duncan stepped up to Layton. "You don't believe Kimball's a prophet any more than I do. Let the healer check it out—it just might put an end to all this and you can start over without Kimball lurking about and playing tricks on your minds."

Layton listened attentively. "I expect your right—someone find the healer." To Eliot, he said, "Eliot, you stand fast until the healer returns. If this is some sort of trick, you'll be the first to get shot."

"Agreed," said Eliot. "Anything, you say just send the healer."

Soon the gate swung open and the compound's healer, a rail thin young man with broad shoulders sauntered through the gate. He stopped abreast of Eliot. "Where is he?"

Eliot pointed. "He's in the tent over there—there's a crowd?"

Twenty-minutes past before the healer returned. Again, he stopped near Eliot. "He died in his sleep of natural causes—I'd say it was most likely a stroke."

Eliot paled at hearing the news. "How can that be—he was God's prophet. God spoke to him—he had a mission."

"He was a psychotic, who in the end died a peaceful death, which is more than I can say for some of those who believed and followed him blindly. Hopefully, he gets his just rewards in hell."

The men above the gate overheard the healer.

Duncan said, "Layton, those are members of you compound. They may have been misguided, but now they're lost and need your help."

Layton turned and watched those milling about the Leader's tent. They seem dazed; in shock and unable to cope. "All right, I'll speak with the elders. They may still want to leave, but in the meantime, they can return to their homes." Duncan nodded and shook his hand.

Later that morning as Duncan's force prepared to leave, the healer stopped by where Duncan, Morgan, and Bernie were drinking coffee and talking. "Good morning, Gentlemen," said the healer.

Good morning to you too, Harrison," said Duncan. Morgan and Bernie nodded as they sipped their coffees.

"I thought I'd stop by before you go." His face held a wry smile. "When I examined Kimball, I noticed strange bruises on his face." He looked directly at Duncan. "Kimball's gone now, and I think it's for the best. It's just as well, he died in his sleep. Any other way could have caused a lot of trouble don't you think, Duncan?"

Duncan reached out and put a hand on Harrison's shoulder. "God moves in mysterious ways, my friend."

"Yes, friend, he does," said the healer.

Chapter 19

Bernie and Dan Fox, less Morgan, along with the other men from Green River left first. Morgan and Farmer's men rode with Duncan, Mary and the New Lovelock militia as far as the 15 north. They were going to collect Farmer and Morgan's Rebecca.

At the junction of the roads, Morgan and Duncan shook hands. "When, I return to Green River, I'll send a telegram to you compound to let your parents know you're alive and well." He smiled at Mary. Is there anything else I should tell them?"

Duncan considered, and he too smiled. "No just that I'll return for a visit soon as I can."

Mary asked, "A visit?"

"I figured after we're married, we'd make our home in New Lovelock. That's where Jane and the twins live. Don't you want to stay close to them, at least for a while?"

"Oh, that would be wonderful, but I do so still want to meet your parents and get your mother's approval."

"Well," said Morgan interrupting. "You'd better Plan on staying a while in Green River, you know Bernie and Lisa will expect it."

"What about you and Rebecca," asked Duncan?

A rare grin appeared on Morgan's face. "She hasn't said yes yet." He reined his horse north and galloped away. He halted and turned back. "I guess we'll be expecting it, too."

***

On their return to New Lovelock, there was a double wedding; Mary and Duncan, and Matt and Jane. Matt and Jane moved in together into her bungalow. Mary and Duncan loaded Sophie and Alice and headed east. They told Marcus, Martha and twins that they expected to return in two months.

On their first night on the trail a pair of golden eyes gleamed at them across the campfire. Duncan eased his hand up to loosen the strap restraining his Glock. The eyes moved closer into the light, it was a female wolf; it was Shadow. With her were five pups, they followed her as she approached. Duncan rose and stepped to greet them. "Hello, Girl. This is a surprise—how've you been?"

She licked his face, sniffed his breath, and whined. "I know, girl, I miss him, too.

END